Assignment Earth

It's a battlefield down there, and very, very dangerous.

Being an angel isn't as easy as you think. There's so much to learn, even when you're brimming with enthusiasm. And, not being perfect, angels can make mistakes – and they do!

Raffael (Raffie to her angelic friends) is desperate to be assigned to Earth. So when she gets her wish, she is determined to do well, even though she keeps getting things wrong. But then she makes a very dangerous mistake. Raffie finds herself suddenly in the middle of a frightening world, the scene of a struggle on a cosmic scale, where forces infinitely stronger than her are playing for the highest stakes imaginable.

Lynda Rose read English at university before qualifying as a barrister. She was later one of the first women to be ordained as both deacon and priest in the Anglican Church and has served at several parishes in and around Oxford. She now writes full-time and has had several fiction and non-fiction books published. She and her husband live in Oxford and have three children. *Assignment Earth* is Lynda's first children's novel.

For Christabel,
to whom the story was first told

ASSIGNMENT EARTH

**Volume I of
The Vortex of Time**

LYNDA ROSE

LION
CHILDREN'S

Text copyright © 2007 Lynda Rose

The moral rights of the author
have been asserted

A Lion Children's Book
an imprint of
Lion Hudson plc
Wilkinson House, Jordan Hill Road,
Oxford OX2 8DR, England
www.lionhudson.com
ISBN: 978-0-7459-6063-0

First edition 2007
1 3 5 7 9 10 8 6 4 2 0

A catalogue record for this book is available
from the British Library

Typeset in 12/15 Elegant Garamond BT
Printed and bound in Great Britain
by Cox and Wyman Ltd, Reading

The text paper used in this book has been made from wood
independently certified as having come from sustainable forests.

Contents

1
A Very Superior Being

It takes a long time to become a fully qualified angel. At least it would do, but of course in heaven they don't use the measurement of time because it's what they call eternity. This is a bit hard to describe, but basically it's a kind of Greenwich Mean Time for the celestial regions, and everything happens all at once and all the time. OK, it doesn't make much sense to mere mortals, but if you're a supernatural being you understand it perfectly. And that was what Raffie – Raffael to give her her full name – was, a very junior angel right at the beginning of her training, and hoping one day, in her wilder flights of fancy, to become a Cherub.

A Cherub, by the way, isn't one of those pudgy kids sitting on clouds that medieval artists were so fond of. No, a Cherub is one of the very highest ranking angels, who have passed all the exams and made it through into the elite corps commanded by Michael. The celestial SAS, if you like. Combat soldiers. But that was a long way off for Raffie. In fact, so long a way off she didn't even dare think about it.

Except, of course, that she did. Endlessly. Her teachers got thoroughly fed up with telling her off for not paying attention. 'Wake up, Raffie!' they'd say. 'What in the name of the Cosmos are you thinking about now?'

But however much they reprimanded her, it didn't do a bit of good. The idea of becoming a Cherub might have seemed about as likely as finding a snowball down in the nether regions (which, of course, as all angels know, is the seventh and lowest level of the heavens and extremely hot), but that didn't stop her imagining herself a fully fledged Watcher – one of the lower ranking warrior grades – bearing four wings and a huge sword. And the place she wanted to go was Earth.

Raffie didn't know much about Earth – in fact she knew almost nothing – but she'd been drawn to it ever since a particularly interesting Cosmology lesson in which they'd looked at the geographical features of different planets. In particular, they'd been studying what Dr Knowitel, their tutor, had called 'the coastline of northern Europe'. This hadn't made much sense to Raffie, but she'd been entranced at how pretty it all was. 'Oooh!' she exclaimed, dancing along a chalky ridge stretched at their feet on the reality imager they happened to be using at the time. 'It's so beautiful. These bits are all frilly and bumpy. And there are pointy things on them!'

'Trees, Raffie,' said Dr Knowitel wearily, not for the first time.

'And what's that stuff?' she exclaimed, completely undeterred, stopping to point at a churning mass of blue to the left, which seemed to be trying to clamber up over the ridge and swallow it.

Dr Knowitel glanced across and replied briefly, 'It's called the sea, angel, as you'd know if you'd been listening.'

'But what is it?' persisted Raffie. 'Why won't it keep still?'

She gave an exploratory poke, and part of the rocky bit under her feet fell away. Dr Knowitel raised his eyes to the higher heavens and exclaimed, 'Oh dear, that's another fjord gone! You're none of you going from here till all that's cleared up, and the imager put back the way it was. You young angels have *got* to learn to be more careful!'

It had been as simple as that. She'd been utterly beguiled by the sheer wonder of it all, and from that moment on she'd been caught, wholly and completely. Every opportunity she got, she buttonholed her teachers (or any passing angel who looked like they might know), and interrogated them about the mysterious planet.

What she didn't realize, however, was that all this interest had drawn the attention of some of the senior teachers responsible for probationer placements (which was what training assignments were called), and one day she was astounded to receive a special summons telling her to report immediately to Gabriel, one of the most senior archangel Seraphs.

This was totally unheard of amongst new entrants and the lower angelic orders, because Gabriel was a *very* important angel, frequently used as a special envoy and emissary by the High King himself, and Raffie was awestruck. As well as a little scared. A summons from an archangel, however, was not something to be ignored, even if you were quaking in your angelic boots, and so Raffie flew immediately up to the higher administrative echelons on the first level and tapped nervously on his door.

The air was very thin up in the topmost celestial regions where Gabriel's office was situated, and Raffie felt a little bit dizzy. Very important looking angels with all sorts of peculiar looking objects in their hands – like digestible and non-digestible scrolls (you could tell by the colour), and huge harps – kept flitting hurriedly backwards and forwards as if engaged on very urgent business. All, however, ignored her and so she just stood there, feeling very small. Then a voice barked out, 'Come!' and very nervously she pushed open the billowy clouds that formed the door and went in.

She found herself in the presence of one of the most beautiful beings she had ever encountered. He was huge, with four mighty wings which seemed to sparkle in a kind of shimmering radiance that flowed from his magnificent body, and he had long dark golden hair and piercing amber eyes. Raffie was transfixed. She had never seen such wings before. They were magnificent, majestic – there was no other way of describing them. In front of him she felt very insignificant, and her own two small, what felt now to be mere sprouts, drooped. The next instant, however, her whole body jerked to attention, because the wonderful angel in front of her suddenly spun round, and his eyes, which seemed to blaze with fire, fixed onto her. 'Stand up straight, Raffael!' he boomed. 'Call yourself an angel? Let's have a bit of right thinking pride here!'

Poor Raffie almost died – except of course that angels can't die, because they're eternal (though they can get hurt and, at worst, lose their individuality). But she felt pretty awful, because no one ever called her 'Raffael' unless she'd done something really wrong and they were cross with her. So her first thought was that she had done something absolutely *dire*, and that maybe she wasn't going to be assigned to training after all, but would have to carry out the rest of her existence churning out nerdy songs with one of the lower grade celestial choirs that seemed forever to be wandering around the universe. In fact, maybe she was going to get thrown out of angel school completely! So she sprang smartly to attention – the way they'd been shown – and gulped.

But the next moment she became aware of the angel looking at her in a strange kind of quizzical, half gentle way that made her feel all funny inside, and she thought that maybe she had been wrong. He didn't really look very angry at all. And then, as if to confirm it, he said quietly, 'I'm told you want to go to Earth!'

Raffie stared at him, dumbstruck. She had the peculiar feeling that she was floating on a huge warm mass of marshmallow. It was actually rather nice. But at the same time, the angel's manner seemed to suggest that no one in their right minds would ever even consider going down to Earth, unless compelled by lesser spotted fire-eating furies (there were some very peculiar beings in the celestial regions). Quite why the desire should seem so strange, Raffie hadn't the remotest idea. For herself, when she gazed at the planet's tiny image in one of the cosmological atlases from the library, it reminded her of a great big marble suspended in space, all milky blue and white. Wholly beautiful! But Gabriel was looking at her in such a peculiar way – sort of admiration and pity at the same time – and she suddenly felt a bit afraid. Maybe Earth wasn't such a good idea after all.

Having got her full attention, however, Gabriel was ploughing on. 'You're going to have to be very careful if you do end up there,' he said admonishingly. 'As training assignments go, Earth is probably the toughest you can get – but I'm told you're absolutely set on it!' He shook his head as if despairing at such folly, and his wings seemed to vibrate and ripple in sympathy, with a soft shushing sound that Raffie found rather distracting. 'If this really is the place you want to go...' he continued. Raffie nodded nervously, and he sighed. 'Then there are certain things you ought to know. It just wouldn't be fair to send you otherwise.'

He gave a nod of his head, the merest kind of shimmer, but Raffie knew she was being told to sit down, and her eyes widened in amazement. To sit in the presence of an archangel! She could hardly believe it. The two things that had so far been drummed into them in training were: first, that you stood at all times; and second, that you spoke only when spoken to... and then as briefly as possible. And yet here was Gabriel, chatting to her as if she were a long lost friend! She gulped and sat down. Gabriel, apparently oblivious of the effect he was having, settled himself opposite.

'A long, long time ago...' he began, choosing his words with care. 'Time is the measurement they use down there, Raffie. Well, a long, long time ago, just after the King first created and activated the whole planet, there was a major revolt led by the Cherub who had been put in overall command of it. He actually tried to mount a leadership challenge, if you can believe it! Naturally, not openly – he'd never have won that way – but by a really despicable underhand plot!'

Raffie's eyes widened. She'd heard something about the 'Great Rebellion' of course, but never any details. It had never even occurred to her that it might have had something to do with Earth. But Gabriel was going on, his expression heavy, and she pulled herself together, listening carefully.

'Yes, a Cherub named Metatron, at the time one of the chief advisors to the King, was appointed Planetary Regent, with special responsibility for terrestrial creature training and security. But he got jealous and imagined he could run the whole show by himself. He gathered together a group of very malign, and completely prohibited, spirits and demons and then he launched a major attack – totally unsuspected beforehand – against the very creatures that the King had had specially designed to maintain the whole system.' He fixed Raffie with a piercing eye and said, 'Mortals, Raffie! You've heard of them?'

Raffie nodded. 'Yes,' she breathed, hardly daring to interrupt the archangel's flow. 'Dr Knowitel told us that they were eternal spirits – like us – but in special bodies adapted to a terrestrial environment. They were an experiment, he said, and they still live on Earth, although they haven't quite developed the way they should have done.'

Gabriel nodded gravely. 'Yes, Raffael,' he agreed. 'You have it exactly. Eternal spirits but in special bodies. Specially made to look after the planet for the term of their terrestrial existence. After that, they were supposed to come back to the heavens and live eternally – just like us. Well, this Cherub – Metatron – tempted them to rebel. Totally beyond his brief of course, and he knew exactly what would happen. But unfortunately they were very young at the time and very foolish. And the result was that they fell for it. They didn't exactly throw in their lot with him, but they were damaged. They lost knowledge of who they are, and Earth's been in chaos ever since. In fact, it's a battlefield down there, and very, very dangerous.'

He paused, then said grimly, 'Which means we *never* allow trainees down there unless we're absolutely sure they can stand it. We don't want any more avoidable casualties, thank you, and I don't usually even consider first years. Your tutors tell me, however, that you're absolutely determined.'

Raffie stared at him glumly, and a feeling of panic flooded her as she wondered what was coming. Would he, or would he not, let her go? She followed the archangel apprehensively with her eyes as he turned and crossed slowly over to the large desk that stood in the corner, drawing across a gleaming scroll that she hadn't noticed before. 'Ye-es,' he said after a moment, picking it up and scrutinizing it carefully. 'Your personal tutor, Lucisel, says you don't seem able to think about anything else... But he also says that I should allow you to go. He says you have qualities which are not immediately obvious.'

Raffie gulped, hardly able to believe her ears and not quite sure whether the last comment was good or bad. Gabriel, however, seemed to find it rather amusing, because the smile grew. Then he cocked his head to one side questioningly and said, 'So then, having heard all this... are you still keen? Do you think you would be able to handle it?'

Raffie didn't need to be asked twice. She nodded her head vigorously, so excited that for a moment she felt she couldn't breathe, and then sprang to her feet. She was going to be allowed to go, she thought ecstatically. It was unbelievable! And all that Gabriel said had only made her even more determined. EARTH... She explored the sound in her mind, totally captivated by it. Gabriel was staring at her quizzically. 'Oooh, yes,' she cried. 'I'm sure I can!' Then she added, 'And I'm not afraid. Honestly, sir... Please, please, do let me go.'

For another instant the archangel looked at her. Raffie felt herself being measured, raked from head to toe, from wing tip to wing tip, and she drew herself up proudly, determined to pass muster, unfurling her now sparkling tiny wings to their fullest extent. Gabriel laughed. 'Very well then,' he replied. 'Go. You'll remain under Lucisel, of course. You probably don't realize it, but he's very experienced down on Earth and a good angel. I wouldn't be at all surprised if he didn't make Cherub one day soon, and if he thinks you can cope, then I'm sure you can.'

He raised a hand to dismiss her, but then stopped as a thought struck him and added, 'Of course, it's mid-term still at the moment for the training college down there. But in the circumstances, and given that you really seem to know very little about actual conditions, I think it might be good for you to get some preliminary experience.' He rubbed his chin reflectively and said, 'I think we'll put you on short term assignment until next term starts with one of the planetary administrative departments. Something easy I think... I know.' His face brightened. 'We'll start you off in Weather!'

2
Close Encounters of the Wet Kind

'Huum,' said Lucisel – or Lucis, as he was more commonly known. 'So you've been assigned to Weather to start with, have you!' He tapped his chin with the scroll Raffie handed him, his face at first solemn, and then gave a huge grin. 'You've got your way then!'

Raffie nodded. She hardly trusted herself to speak. She felt so proud. For the first time since her meeting with Gabriel, she looked at Lucis properly and felt a start of surprise. Always before she had thought her tutor angel to be indescribably grand. In fact, she had felt terrified when she first met him, and with good reason, because Lucis was a towering three metres, and his four wings must have had a wing span of about seven. He was one of the all-seeing 'Watcher' angels, which meant he had unflagging 360 degree vision, which Raffie found slightly disturbing in itself, and she had been told he stood guard on one of the gates of heaven when not doing tutor duty. Which meant, she knew, that he had to be pretty nifty on his wings, because sometimes all sorts of unpleasant things tried to get in.

Like Metatron and his rebelling spirits, she thought now, peering at Lucis with a new respect. But all the same, and despite the shimmering radiance that seemed to surround him, he was still nowhere near as utterly and awe-inspiringly magnificent as Gabriel, and Raffie felt oddly comforted by that fact. Gabriel, it was true, had been extremely kind and had clearly done his best to make her feel at ease, but all the same, to poor Raffie, he had given off such an aura of electrifying power that she had felt as about significant as a lesser tufted proton, which in Earth terms is about the size of a gnat.

As if reading her thoughts, Lucis smiled again and said sympathetically, 'Quite an experience, isn't it? Meeting one of the archangels. I was a squab, a couple of aeons more advanced than you maybe, and just commissioned into the Watchers when I first met him. We'd had some action, I remember, out on one of the black holes. Bit nasty actually – a couple of planets got sucked in before we could prevent it, but we managed to block off the gap. In the end. And afterwards Gabriel summoned us all up to see him. Said he wanted to commend us for our valiant action… It was only when we got there and met him that we realized he'd actually been there too. Only we hadn't seen him at the time.' He sighed, shaking his head, and then said, 'That's the way with archangels, you know. There are often times when you don't know they're there. But they are! The trick is to learn to recognize the signs.'

'Gosh,' said Raffie faintly. She stared at him, awestruck. She was beginning to realize just how much there was to learn. 'What signs?' she asked after a minute, feeling that something was required of her. 'How did you find out he'd been there? Did he tell you?'

Lucis shook his head. 'No,' he said firmly. 'He'd never have done that. Code of honour and all that. No, when we got there we noticed he was wounded. That was what first put us on to it. And later Michael, you know, our

Commander-in-Chief, he buttonholed us and told us what had happened. Apparently two or three of them had come out to help us, because we were new and they'd heard we were in trouble. We'd actually been pretty close to losing, although we didn't realize it at the time. But then the AA arrived… archangels,' he explained, seeing Raffie's look of bewilderment, 'and suddenly everything seemed to change. We started to get on top of things. We hadn't a clue what was going on, of course. We just thought that the Enemy were getting tired and were giving up… We thought we'd been lucky.' He grimaced at the memory, then laughed and said briskly, 'Anyway, enough of that. It says here,' he pointed to the scroll, 'that I've got to get you over to Weather Station 3.' He winked. 'That's a good one, that is. There's an old angel runs it called Drizzlewobbel, and you'll have fun with him. A little odd, there's no denying. Can be a bit testy, but a spirit of gold! He's very up on global weather patterns, and you'll have a complete view of the whole planet. Jolly good start actually, because you'll get a feel for the entire place without becoming bogged down in anything too nasty. And in fact, some of the things they do, like sunsets and rainbows, are really extremely pretty. You can get to be very creative down there.'

Lucis blasted off into space, and Raffie hastily took to her wings in pursuit. She didn't want to get left behind, not now. They plummeted through the upper stratosphere at a rate that soon had Raffie's head swimming, Lucis leading the way with a trail of blazing light that fanned out behind him like a beacon. 'People down on Earth will think I'm a UFO,' he called cheerfully over his shoulder as they emerged from behind a cloud and shot over the south Atlantic. 'They love that kind of thing down there. Always on the lookout for aliens! A band of Seraphs was spotted flying in formation over Beijing in China a while back. Made the national papers. They thought it was a space ship!'

Raffie, panting to keep up in the rear, could only nod. She really must do some wing building exercises, she decided, or she'd never be able to survive at this rate. Lucis was simply too fast. They arrived moments later in the twinkling of a celestial eye, which is the kind of thing that happens with eternal time, and Raffie found herself standing gasping on the threshold of a huge building that seemed to be made of ice. It was very pretty; the battlemented turrets that rose up before them stood out against the azure, cloudless sky like the frosted decorations of a giant cake. Bemused, Raffie reached out a hand to touch the walls, and discovered that they were vibrating gently, resonating with a low hum that seemed to give off colour, sometimes blue and sometimes green, but always with a faint translucent shimmer that made the surface seem to shift and dance. She rubbed her eyes and looked harder, and beyond she saw what looked to be dozens of winged figures, flitting backwards and forwards like moths round a flame, all looking very busy.

'So is this where they control all the weather?' she asked uncertainly.

'No, no,' said Lucis. He appeared preoccupied and was looking round as if in search of someone. 'Only the weather for this area of the Cosmos, that's all. I thought I made that clear.' At the same moment he gave a loud explosive 'aah!' as if he had located the object of his search, and set off briskly towards the main entrance, which swung open at their approach. Once again Raffie found she had to rush to keep up.

'There are nine weather stations in all,' continued Lucis, not even bothering to look behind to make sure she was there, 'dotted throughout the Cosmos, and all with special areas of responsibility. Drizzlewobbel is in charge of all the weather for this particular part of the solar system, but you've only been assigned to help with Earth – as you asked.'

They passed through the main entrance and Raffie was surprised now to find that the ground underfoot felt warm. Lucis led the way down the long corridor that opened off the far side of the vaulted hall, and then on through into the circular transparent-floored room that lay at the end. The view was stunning and Raffie gasped. She found that the whole Earth was stretched out beneath them, continent merging seamlessly into continent, the smallest speck of vegetation clearly visible. Towering waterfalls plunged into tree-filled ravines. The polar regions cracked and creaked gently under an azure sky. Barren rock filled deserts crawled their way exhausted into thin looking oases and gasped for refreshment. 'How is this possible?' she breathed, awestruck. 'It's beautiful!'

Lucis smiled and nodded to where a group of angels skimmed and fluttered across the room, moving busily between various levers and controls, pushing and adjusting, keeping everything in check. 'It's possible,' he said, 'because they're looking after it. This is their job –

despite what sometimes seem the best efforts of men and women down there to sabotage it.'

Raffie stared around wide-eyed, and was delighted to see that a couple of angels seemed hardly more advanced than herself. Lucis, however, singled out a rather decrepit-looking angel with spectacles and a long white beard, and headed towards him. 'Drizzle!' he yelled out happily, 'A moment! I have a new recruit for you.'

The angel he addressed paused in what he was doing (which, to Raffie, didn't seem very much) and looked round. His long, papery hand had just curled around a heavy-looking, copper lever, and he was in the act of slowly moving it backwards, but at Lucis' shout he stopped and looked annoyed. 'Tck!' he said. 'Don't go startling me like that. You'll make me cause a hurricane over Skegness!'

Lucis looked crestfallen. 'Sorry,' he muttered. 'Wasn't thinking. It's just that I've brought someone new to join you.'

He stood back, gesturing towards Raffie with a now much more restrained flick of his wing, and the young angel suddenly found herself the object of close and rather uncomfortable scrutiny. Drizzlewobbel stared at her as if he could not quite believe his eyes, then carefully shut off the machine, removed his glasses, polished them and then replaced them on the tip of his long thin nose. 'A new recruit,' he enunciated. 'What are you talking about? I haven't had any notification of this.'

Lucis looked slightly sheepish but nevertheless attempted to smile seraphically and said quickly, 'No, no, you wouldn't have, that's right. I've brought all the

21

paperwork with me. Thought it would save time.' Then he stood back, clearly not wishing to pursue this line of conversation, and pushed Raffie forwards into the space between them. 'She's very keen,' he added encouragingly.

Drizzlewobbel gave Lucis a long look. It was the kind of look that said, 'Don't think I don't know what you're up to, sunbeam. This is totally out of line. You know I've got to have my proper paperwork or I'm not playing. Take her away and send me a memo!' But to Raffie's surprise – and immense relief – he actually said none of this. Instead, after a moment, he merely sighed heavily and then swivelled his eyes back towards her and said with despair, 'She's very young. Are you sure you haven't made a mistake?'

Lucis ruffled like an insulted hen. 'No I haven't,' he said firmly. 'I have the authorization signed by Gabriel himself. Raffael has been assigned to you to learn specifically about weather tracking and seasonal variations on planet Earth before being sent to attend training school.'

Drizzlewobbel sniffed loudly. To Raffie the noise seemed a reproach, summing up all his aversion to administrative mismanagement. 'Oh very well,' he said ungraciously. 'If I must have her! But I really do resent the way I'm expected to take all these young angels and train them up, and then see them move on. Not a bit of good to me! As soon as they've learned anything, off they go. Seems to me that I get all the bother and none of the benefit!'

He turned away, still muttering to himself and, behind his back, Lucis gave Raffie a broad wink. 'Don't worry,' he mouthed at her. 'Bark's much worse than his bite.' Then aloud he said, 'So I'll leave her with you then, Drizzle, shall I? Can I just ask you to sign this?' He unfurled the scroll and pushed it towards the chief weather angel, and from his pocket whipped out a quill pen, and then another, and another, and another, till he was holding four in all. 'Here… here, here… and here,' he said, indicating the spots on the parchment and holding up a different pen each time.

Drizzlewobbel glared at him, but obediently took the pens and began to sign. Peering over his shoulder, Raffie noticed that his writing was long and spidery, and as he formed the letters they shimmered and danced in a myriad of colours, like a rainbow having difficulty keeping still. It was very pretty.

As soon as he'd finished, Lucis deftly gathered up the pens, refurled the scroll and returned the lot to one of his capacious pockets. 'Well, I'll be off then,' he announced cheerfully. He looked pleased. 'Raffie, I'll be back to pick you up in about four of the Earth's weeks. Good luck!' And with that, he disappeared.

Drizzlewobbel winced. 'Oh I do wish he wouldn't do that!' he said testily, as the air shimmered and then righted itself. 'I find it so disturbing when these angels appear and disappear without a by your leave. It's so rude! Here on Weather we never do that.'

'That's because you never go outside,' floated down a voice.

Drizzlewobbel's scowl grew. 'And I hate that even more!' he bellowed, shaking a fist up towards the last remaining trace of a glimmer in the air. 'Kindly have the decency to stand in front of me when you talk to me, and don't address me from the other side of the firmament.'

A low laugh was the only answer to this, and Drizzlewobbel shook his head, then turned and stared at Raffie, once again pushing his glasses up his nose. 'So,' he said mournfully, and as if this were somehow an aberration that needed to be addressed, 'it said on the delivery note that you'd specially requested to train on Earth. Any particular reason why?'

Raffie gulped at being addressed in this way. 'Not really,' she replied, hastily trying to gather her wits – and failing dismally. 'I just thought it looked nice, that's all.'

'Nice!' Drizzlewobbel repeated the word as if he had never heard it before. In fact he didn't so much repeat it as declaim it in tones of horror, as if it were the kind of word that should never be mentioned in polite society, not if you knew what was good for you. 'Nice!' he repeated again. 'You have here before you one of the wonders of the Cosmos... and you call it NICE!'

Raffie blinked. 'Er... yes,' she said.

Drizzlewobbel looked as if he were about to explode. 'My dear young angel!' he cried, 'Earth is many things. It is sublime, wonderful, tragic, cataclysmic... but one of the things it most assuredly is not is NICE. The King does not do NICE! The King does EXQUISITE. He does SUPERB! He does MATCHLESS... But he never does just "nice"!' Having exploded in this way, however, Drizzlewobbel seemed to feel rather better, because he sniffed again (scornfully, it was true) and said, 'Anyway, welcome. I hope you'll be very happy here.'

Raffie was stunned. She didn't quite know what to make of Weather Station 3. But, over the coming Earth days, she found that, if Drizzlewobbel was at times ferocious, he was also an excellent and patient teacher and, guided by him, she very quickly began to learn how to control and manipulate the weather patterns down on the planet below. In fact, she proved so good that, early one Earth morning, Drizzlewobbel said, 'Raffie, I'm going to put you in charge of seasonal variation this morning. It's winter in the polar regions, but summer in the Sahara, and there's a rather fine spring happening over England. I want you to follow this chart here and fine-tune the worldwide weather patterns so that they all fit. It's not at all difficult. Just follow the pre-programmed red and green arrows the way you've been taught.'

Raffie felt rather proud. Only a short while ago and she had never even heard of things like 'Sahara' and 'polar regions', but now she knew where they were instantly, locating them without the slightest trace of difficulty on the worldwide vistagram spread out beneath her feet. 'All right,' she said, and was rewarded by a twinkle in Drizzlewobbel's old eyes.

'You think you can manage it?' he asked.

She nodded.

'Right then.' He handed over the chart he had taken down from the wall behind the main control panel and gave a huge yawn. 'In that case, I'm going to go and get a spot of shut eye. I haven't had a sleep for a hundred and fifty Earth years!'

He turned and shuffled off and, with a feeling of horror, Raffie realized she was going to be left alone. It was oddly quiet that morning. All the other angels seemed to have been called out on assignment because there was a huge hurricane over the Eastern Seaboard of the United States, and it kept trying to uncurl itself into the Caribbean. Drizzlewobbel had got very cross because he'd said you couldn't just let hurricanes do what they wanted willy nilly, but the hurricane hadn't listened, and so he'd dispatched a major band of angels to sort it out. But, Raffie suddenly realized, the result was that she was alone.

She looked around uncertainly, suppressing an urgent desire to call Drizzlewobbel back, and then felt ashamed. Poor Drizzlewobbel was actually rather nice when you got to know him, and he did look very tired. She couldn't possibly deprive him of his sleep. And besides, what could go wrong? He'd said himself that all she had to do was follow the arrows on the chart. She gave herself a mental shake, and then turned back towards the control panel and began to scan the intricate sheet clasped in her hands.

Her heart sank. For all Drizzlewobbel's assurance, it was like nothing she had ever seen before. There were all kinds of funny hieroglyphs and weird signs, and things seemed to cross-connect and then end in brackets, with the words 'To be continued later' written above them in Drizzlewobbel's rather untidy scrawl, but there didn't seem very many arrows at all. Poor Raffie felt lost. She had never been much good at mathematics up in angel school, it was true, but this was something else again. She could make neither head nor tail of it.

She turned the chart this way and that, trying to see if it made any more sense if she held it the other way up; for a second she thought it did, because there was a little bit that she thought looked distinctly like Portugal when she shut one eye, with a green arrow going off to the left. When she looked at the chart more closely, however, she saw that written over it was 'Seasonal snowstorm, temp –21 °C' and so she decided that had to be wrong, because she knew Portugal was warm at the season they were in. 'Oh dear,' she muttered, turning the chart again. 'He said it was easy.'

She cast a despairing glance down at the transparent floor and then decided to walk all around it, holding the chart over various bits to see if anywhere seemed to fit that way. She had never really done this before, always too busy with the detailed duties Drizzlewobbel assigned her, but now she discovered how very exciting it all was. If she looked very closely, she found out that she could actually see people and animals all over the ground. She had had no idea how teeming with life it all was, and she began to look out for various species that she had come across back in the books in the library that she had pored over for so long and which had always delighted her. 'Gosh,' she thought, 'that funny looking thing there must be a horse. And that's a lion, surely, or is it a tiger?' She searched her mind, trying to remember whether lions had stripes or a mane, and then got diverted when she saw a huge great slimy thing, half in and half out of a river just below her feet. 'What on Earth's that?' she thought. 'Not sure I'm too keen on that. It looks a bit cross!' And then, as she moved on, she came across some large beautiful white furry creatures, sitting shivering on a cap of ice. 'Wow!' she said aloud. 'They're wonderful! But they look so cold.'

She consulted the chart again and decided that they must be in the region called Equator. But that was rather odd, she thought, scanning it intently, because the chart said the temperature ought to be 40°C, which sounded to Raffie to be quite hot. The poor creatures down below, however, seemed distinctly chilly. And, to her eyes, they didn't look too happy about it either.

She swivelled the chart round and then laid it on the floor, trying to check whether or not she really had got the right bit and what the arrows were doing. But whichever way she looked at it, she still felt convinced that the land beneath her feet was the Equator, and that the temperature the animals were experiencing was therefore wrong.

'I wonder if Drizzlewobbel has made a mistake,' she said to herself at last. 'After all, he did say he was really tired. And those poor animals down there look so fed up. They're probably wondering why it's not hot. I wonder if I ought to go and get him, or if I ought just to try and put it right myself.'

She peered at the chart once again, and then wandered back to the controls and stared down at all the different buttons and levers. Yes, there was the temperature regulation lever, and by flicking the dial she could check the area of Earth she had just been standing over. She reached out a hand and turned the dial – just to see what the temperature actually was – and gave a gasp of surprise. Yes, it definitely said –21°C. Far too cold for the Equator. She was now seriously worried. Just then a low snore rumbling into the room from behind told her that Drizzlewobbel was well and truly asleep. She couldn't wake him up, not now. She came to a sudden decision. He obviously had made a mistake because he was so very tired. She would put it right. Quickly she reached out and began very slowly to pull up the temperature lever. The needle quivered and then began to rise: $-19°$... $-16°$... $-8°$... $-1°$... $16°$... $38°$... $40°$. She thought she'd give them an extra degree just to make up for all the unexpected cold.

When at last she stood back, wiping a hand across her forehead, she discovered that she was sweating slightly. Moving the lever had been a lot harder than she had expected. She went back over to look down and check on her handiwork, and was pleased to see that the ice was melting rapidly and that the huge white furry creatures seemed to be leaping around with joy. 'Good,' she murmured, 'Drizzlewobbel will be really pleased when he sees this.'

Next, she walked across to a yellowish area that seemed to be filled with a lot of rocks, and again consulted her chart. 'Now, if that was the Equator,' she muttered to herself, 'this must be... Brazilian rainforest.' She stared at it with puzzlement, wondering what had happened to the trees, and then realized that there were men and women poking at the ground and looking a bit glum. 'Everything seems to have died,' she said to herself. 'That's a bit odd. According to the arrows on the chart, it ought to be raining at the moment.' She walked over the Earth slowly and discovered another bit that she thought looked like Great Britain, because it was an island and a funny shape and there was a big lump of rock in the sea on its left. 'Hum,' she said to herself, 'there's an awful lot of rain over that funny bit hanging on the side. They look as if they've got too much. I wonder if that's because the hurricane squad have pushed all the water across the Atlantic.' She stooped down for a closer look, and decided that the land beneath her feet was definitely having too much rain. There seemed to be floods everywhere, and the few people out and about all carried umbrellas and looked miserable. 'Hum,' she said again. 'I know what I'll do. I'll take some of the rain from here, and transfer it to the Brazilian rainforest, and then they'll be getting all the rain they should, and the people of the British Isles will be having a nice heatwave to make up for all that wet!'

She went back to the panel and flicked a few more switches, and was pleased to see a rainstorm gather quickly over the sandy bit that she had decided was rainforest. The next moment a huge bank of clouds gathered and then exploded into torrential rain. The people down below all seemed surprised and then began to leap and dance around wildly, some of them flinging themselves into the gathering pools of water and beginning to swim. 'Good,' said Raffie, pleased. 'They look as if they're really enjoying it. That's much better. I hope the trees don't take too long to grow.'

At that moment, a strangled sound behind her made her spin round. She found Drizzlewobbel standing behind her, an expression of horror on his wrinkled old face. In fact, he was so upset that his long white hair seemed to be standing up on end and his wings had gone into spasm. 'Raffie!' he blurted out. 'What on Earth have you done?'

The question should perhaps more properly have been, 'What have you done on Earth?', but Raffie was too astonished to notice any defects of grammar. Her superior seemed almost apoplectic with rage. He was dancing up and down over 'the Equator', moaning and wringing his hands, while the large white creatures underneath hopped around in what almost seemed like a mirror image of his behaviour on the tiny patch of ice below, which was all that was left of the huge floe they had been sitting on.

'I just adjusted the temperature for the Equator,' she replied uncertainly. 'I thought the monkeys looked cold.'

'Monkeys!' spluttered Drizzlewobbel. 'What monkeys? They're not monkeys, you silly angel. They're polar bears. And you've just destroyed their home.'

'What?' Raffie felt an icy trickle of dread. 'But the chart...' she began.

'The chart...' echoed Drizzlewobbel. He snatched it from her hand and turned it round, then stabbed the top with a shaking finger. 'It's not the Equator, it's the Arctic, and you've made the ice cap melt. We're going to have a major flood in Europe. Thousands of creatures could die. We must put it all back immediately!'

He pushed her out of the way, and began feverishly to spin dials, press buttons and turn wheels. Appalled, Raffie watched as the polar bears/monkeys began to stop dancing and running round each other, and settled back onto the ice. 'We *must* reverse the process,' muttered Drizzlewobbel distractedly, snapping the controls onto 'super freeze'. 'What else have you done, Raffie?'

Raffie didn't feel quite so confident now. 'I made it rain over the Brazilian rainforest,' she said nervously.

'Rain, over Brazil?' repeated Drizzlewobbel incredulously. 'But you didn't need to, it was raining already.'

Raffie took her courage in both hands. 'Yes, I know it was supposed to be,' she said. 'But it wasn't. When I looked there was a drought. I thought you must have made a mistake. So I took some of the rain that shouldn't have been over the British Isles, and sent it there.'

Agitatedly, as if the floor had inexplicably become very hot, Drizzlewobbel danced across and looked down at the spot Raffie indicated. 'That's the Sahara,' he said. 'And you've caused major flooding. They can't take too much rain all in one go.' He gave a groan and sank to his knees. 'So we're not just going to have Europe and North America under water, we're going to have Africa swamped too!' He slapped a hand to his forehead and exclaimed, 'Ten Earth minutes rest, and I come back to global disaster! How in heaven's name am I going to explain all this to the Council? We must put it right!'

He crossed back to the desk and pulled another lever. Miraculously it stopped raining over the Sahara and the sun came out. Just then, the hurricane squadron returned. They were drenched, and some of them seemed to have lost quite a few feathers. 'You wouldn't believe the weather down there!' said the first as they came back in through the doors. 'I've never seen anything like it. The whole world seems to have gone mad!'

Drizzlewobbel sighed and stared across at Raffie. 'No,' he said. 'Not the whole world… just one of my helpers.'

3
Mopping Up

Raffie was sent to the Rain Room. 'You've caused this mess,' said Drizzlewobbel ominously. 'You can help clear it up.'

Chastened, she collected a bucket and mop from the Cosmic Supply Office and made her way down to the large open-ended chamber that was situated on the very lowest level of the station, and from where all the weather, ordered by Control, was poured out onto the Earth. It was the most peculiar place that Raffie had ever seen. All along one wall were huge tanks, with hosepipes and sprinklers attached. On Earth it would be impossible to imagine such huge containers, all so close together, and all squashed into one room, because each one was bigger than an oil refinery, and just about as untidy. But these of course were up in the heavens, and so all the rules about size and space that normally apply were simply not relevant. Even Raffie, however, was impressed and she stared round, amazed.

Facing the first line of tanks, she discovered a row of even bigger, and certainly far stranger-looking, machines – all labelled with things like 'Thunder Claps', 'Sheet Lightning', 'Hurricane Force 2', 'Tornadoes – Various'... The list went on and on, and her eyes grew round. It had never occurred to her before to wonder how the weather was actually produced.

However, she suddenly realized that the space in between the two lines of tanks was awash with water, and that all the young angels who worked down there were scurrying around like demented ants, trying desperately to mop up the mess. Raffie stood in the doorway, blinking and wondering what to do. Then a young angel, hurrying past, paused and said, 'Hello. You're looking a bit lost, can I help?'

Raffie stared at him. He was, she judged, in angel terms only a little bit older than herself, but he was much bigger – tall and muscular-looking, and with two powerful wings that looked as if they were already well on the way to being fully grown. He looked like a Cherub in the making and he reminded her a little bit of Lucis because, like her mentor, his face was open and cheery, and he had long shining blue-black hair. Unlike Lucis, however, his hair was tied roughly back in a ponytail to keep it out of the way, and he looked distinctly dishevelled.

Raffie herself was a much smaller kind of angel, with pale silvery skin that had a kind of shimmering glow, and long red hair that fell in a mass of glowing curls on her shoulders. The two looked at each other and the boy grinned. Raffie realized that she had seen him before. He had been up in the weather room when she first arrived. 'I've seen you before, haven't I?' she asked impulsively. 'You were helping Drizzlewobbel when Lucis brought me.'

The boy looked pleased. 'Yes, that's right,' he replied. 'I thought you hadn't noticed me. You're Raffael, aren't you?' He put down the bucket he was carrying and held out a dripping hand. 'I'm Joshuel – Josh, for short – and you're the creative genius who caused all this mess, aren't you?'

Raffie was embarrassed, but she swallowed and grasped the offered hand – reminding herself that humility was a virtue even among angels, and grateful at least that he was talking to her. She had thought that, after all that had happened, she might be ignored or excluded. The next moment, however, a warm kind of sticky goo seemed to transfer itself to her fingers and then wound itself lovingly around her hand and lower arm. 'Yuck!' she exclaimed, abruptly letting go of Josh's hand and trying vainly to pull the stuff off. But it was no good. The harder she tried, the more determined the slime seemed to be to attach itself to her, and she suddenly found she had great long strings of the stuff stretching between either hand.

Josh watched her with interest. 'Ah, sorry about that,' he remarked casually. 'I didn't think. The equatorial rain solution overflowed into blizzards and tornadoes, you see. It's horrible to get off once it mixes. Makes adhesive sludge... that's one of the reasons it's such a mess down here. We're finding it very difficult to shift, even with Drizzlewobbel's high density all-purpose weather solvent, but until we get it cleared away we haven't a hope of getting the weather back to normal on Earth. We've had a blizzard over Jamaica for the last three days because we can't get close enough to the snow vat to turn it off.'

Trying to wipe her fingers against the nearest available hard surface – in this case the wall, which only succeeded in sticking her to it – Raffie paused, then said desperately, 'I'm really sorry to hear about Jamaica, but how in heaven do I get this stuff off? It seems to be spreading.'

Josh laughed. 'Here,' he said, relenting. He held out a cloth which he took from the belt at his waist and said,

'Rub your hands on this. It will stop it from spreading and begin to dissolve it.' Then, as she gratefully began to wipe her hands, he went on, 'You can see what we're up against. Your rearrangement of Earth's weather system has given us a bit of a cosmic crisis up here too. Drizzlewobbel's having to get us all to work flat out to try to get it straight. But once we've got it cleaned up up here, then we'll be able to go down to Earth and mop up down there too.'

Pulling away the last remaining strands of slime, Raffie paused. This was a development she hadn't even considered. 'You mean we're going to have to go and clean up down on Earth too?' she asked incredulously.

'Of course,' he replied easily, 'once we've got everything sorted out up here. After all, they'll never get it straight by themselves.'

Josh introduced her to Libertybel, another tall angel, but with blond hair this time and a long robe covered with brightly coloured stars and stripes. He looked rather fed up, but his sleeves were rolled back, and he was energetically dispensing dusters, sponges and large bottles bearing the label 'Drizzlewobbel's all-purpose weather solvent' to a long line of angels, who no sooner seemed to have received their allocation than they were back, asking for more. 'Brought another helper, Bel,' announced Josh cheerfully, pushing his way to the head of the queue and thrusting her forward. 'She's called Raffael, and she's the one who caused all this mess.'

Heaving across a fresh box of sponges, Libertybel – or Bel, as he seemed to be more commonly known – eyed her narrowly. 'Oh, so it was you, was it?' he drawled. 'I heard it was a rookie who had caused the mayhem. What were you trying to do? Flood the entire planet?' His eyes narrowed. 'In case you didn't know, that already happened a few Earth millennia ago.'

Offended by his tone, Raffie bristled and glared at him. 'I wasn't trying to flood anything,' she retorted frostily. 'I just couldn't read the chart, that was all. It didn't make sense.'

Another couple of angels, busily mopping up nearby, overheard and one called out, 'Didn't make a lot of sense to me either, dear. I was in Norway, and we had a tornado and a heatwave both at the same time. You should have seen what it did to the fjords! There was ice flying around everywhere, and then it melted. The poor old reindeer didn't know what to do with themselves.'

There were murmurs of agreement all round, and then others began to say what they'd experienced too. 'I was in Hawaii,' said one excitedly. 'The surfers tried to lay their boards end to end to make a bridge across the snow.'

'I was in the Russian grasslands,' added another. 'It's winter down there at the moment and really bitter, but the temperature suddenly shot up to 43° degrees Centigrade. There were people fainting everywhere…'

Aghast at the tales of disaster that seemed to come from all sides, Raffie hung her head. She thought she might never be able to live this down. But then it hit her that the effects were so awful that she might not be allowed to begin training either. She might be allowed just to help clear up and then be sent back in disgrace, with the recommendation from Drizzlewobbel that she never be allowed near a planet ever again.

The thought was so horrendous that she went pale (a rather extraordinary sight in an angel); Josh, catching her sudden change of expression, laughed and said, 'Cheer up! We all make mistakes... Although,' he added reflectively, 'not always perhaps on quite such a magnificent scale... but we'll get it put right. In the end. Drizzlewobbel's pretty good, you know.'

'Yeah!' Libertybel thrust a sponge roughly towards Raffie, at the same time depositing a bottle of cleaner none too gently into the bucket she was carrying. 'If Drizzle was going to send you back, you'd have gone already. So stop feeling sorry for yourself and get a move on with helping us clear up!'

Slightly comforted, though still feeling rather edgy, Raffie set to work. But it was all so strange to her that, try as she might, she kept on making mistakes. At last, after she had dropped three sponges down one of the waste disposal tubes that filtered the weather station's drainage vents and was blocked with sludge, Josh took pity on her and said, 'Look, just follow me around for a while and watch. Then we'll mop up together.' Then he added under his breath, 'It'll be safer that way.'

By the end of the shift – which in Earth time, as Raffie later discovered, was about ten months – the Rain Room was beginning to look considerably straighter. All the hoses and sprinklers leading from the various machines had been cleaned and straightened out, and were once more working properly, and the floor area between the two rows of tanks was, if not exactly shining, at least now clear of sludge. It was so clean that, through its surface, Raffie could now dimly make out the curve and outline of the Earth far below. From her vantage point high above, the planet's surface looked relatively calm – though whether that was due to the work of clean-up teams already down there, or their own efforts, she wasn't sure. Either way it was a relief, and she felt her spirits lift slightly.

As they were putting away the last sponges and mops, and stowing the buckets in a corner ready to be returned altogether to Supplies, Drizzlewobbel himself appeared with his second-in-command, Flurripurel, and did a quick tour of inspection. 'Not bad, not bad,' he muttered, poking and prodding the hoses and peering at the various attachments. 'At least it will, I think, do until we've finished cleaning up the mess left behind on Earth.' He gave a curt nod to Flurripurel and said, 'Arrange rotas, please, for extra emergency teams to go to all designated areas. I want scorched Earth removed and all the last areas of deluge mopped up.'

He swept round in a great arc, wings fanning out in what looked to be a ruffle of distaste as he stepped gingerly forward across the still-damp floor. His eye fell on Raffie. 'Ah!' he said, pulling up short. 'Yes...' He stared at her, and under his gaze Raffie began to wish that the floor would open up and swallow her. But it didn't, and at last the ancient Weather angel said reprovingly, 'I trust you now at least appreciate something of the extent of your folly.'

Raffie wriggled uncomfortably, acutely aware of all the other angels staring at her, and mumbled, 'Yes, I do... I'm very sorry, sir... your honour.'

'Pardon?' snapped Drizzlewobbel, cupping a hand around his ear and straining forward, as if he found it difficult to hear.

'I'm very sorry,' repeated Raffie more loudly.

'Sorry!' boomed Drizzlewobbel. 'Sorry?' His expression seemed to imply that she jolly well would be, if he had anything to do with it. But then, after a moment, his face seemed to relax and he said more gently, 'Yes, well, you won't make that mistake again in a hurry, I'm sure. We're all allowed one mistake at least.'

Raffie could hardly believe her ears. She had still been half expecting him to say that now she could go, and not come back! But Drizzlewobbel had not finished yet. He cast a critical look around and his eye fell on Josh, still hovering just behind with Libertybel. 'Hu-um,' he said reflectively, stroking his chin. 'Yes, you two might do.' He crooked a long finger, beckoning them towards him, and said, 'Joshuel, Libertybel, come here.'

The two angels jumped smartly to attention, furling their wings, and came to stand beside Raffie. Drizzlewobbel looked at them thoughtfully, and Raffie had the impression that he was debating something in his mind. Then he said abruptly, 'There's a messy little problem down in the Snowdonia area of Wales. It's not too difficult, but it is *very* wet. I want you two to go and sort it out. It should be well within your capabilities... and I want you to take Raffael with you. Show her what to do, and let her have a glimpse of what Earth's really like.' He turned away then suddenly glanced back and barked over his shoulder, 'And don't let her get into trouble!'

Then there was a little flurry of cold air, and he was gone – but not before, to Raffie's surprise, he cast one last look over towards her... and gave a broad wink. Raffie was so taken aback that her mouth dropped open. She thought she had maybe imagined it. After all, it was ridiculous, the idea of someone like Drizzlewobbel winking at her. But she had no time to explore the idea, because Libertybel gave a great whoop of delight and exclaimed, 'Wales! Can you believe it! We're going to get to sort out a problem all by ourselves.'

'An easy problem,' said Flurripurel dismissively, overhearing. Then he bent his head to peer at the thick sheaf of papers in his hand and Raffie heard him mutter, 'Really, young angels these days! No sense of decorum.'

But Libertybel was unabashed. 'We're being sent on our own,' he said to Josh, ecstatically. 'Unbelievable…'

'Yeah,' Josh agreed. He looked just as excited. 'And we're going to take Raffael too.'

They both turned and stared at her, and Josh said speculatively, 'You know, you can't be in that much trouble if old Drizzle's going to let you go Earthside. It's amazing. I thought you'd be grounded for an Earth millennium at least!'

They set out as soon as they had eaten a light meal of angel cakes and whipped nectar, washed down with sparkling ambrosia. All of the angels who were to go had been assigned specific ground duties, and the ones remaining looked at them with envy. 'Everyone likes to see action,' explained Josh. 'It's what we're all being trained for, but it's only rarely that any of us gets to go out on active service. You're supposed to have experience for that kind of thing, you see, and most of us are first grade and aren't licensed to carry weapons.'

'Yeah,' chimed in Bel, his tones edged with disgust. 'Which is why we only get to have lightning rods, and not swords, even though we don't know what we might meet!'

He made a feint, as if lunging with a huge sword, and Josh laughed. 'Better hurry up and become a Watcher, if you want one of those.' Then, seeing Raffie's confusion, he explained, 'Only commissioned angels get to carry swords. Non-graduates are only allowed lightning rods, which are basically designed as lights, but can also in an emergency be used for defensive purposes.' He smiled. 'That's not very likely of course, given we're only on clearing duty, but you never know... Although even if it were dangerous, I think most of us would still want to go. Only of course they can't send everyone, because there always has to be a full quota of angels manning the station up here, just in case anything goes wrong.'

Libertybel gave a hoot of laughter. 'That's probably why Drizzle's sending Raffael with us. He doesn't want any more cosmic disasters!'

Raffie sniffed, but she felt that on the whole she deserved that. And besides, she was so happy at the idea of being a part of one of the terrestrial clean-up teams that it was impossible to feel angry for long. 'Raffie,' she said firmly, deciding to ignore the insult. 'If we're going to be working together, you'd better call me Raffie.'

4
The Cottage

Raffie, Josh and Libertybel were issued their rods, and flew out just as the bright aureole of the sun was beginning to show over the rim of the Earth. Shafts of brilliant light shot through what seconds before had been the inky darkness of space, transforming it in an instant. 'Morning Star!' shouted Libertybel as the planet Venus appeared on the horizon. He plummeted ecstatically through the air and turned an unintended somersault, wings outstretched. 'Isn't it great?'

He looked like a great lolloping puppy, bounding around excitedly as soon as it was freed from its leash; Josh, flying more soberly behind, scowled at this display of aerobatics and clutched the orders given them by Flurripurel more firmly in his hand. 'Come on, Bel,' he said impatiently. 'Stop fooling, will you!'

There was something steady and comforting about Josh, Raffie thought, glancing at him as they flew along. It was as if he had long ago assessed the Cosmos and taken a decision on where he stood, and would not now be deflected by anything that might try to draw him astray. The powerful beat of his wings sounded like a huge, steady engine throbbing relentlessly through the air and, watching him and Libertybel now flying side by side, Raffie suddenly felt rather insignificant and small. She just wasn't built the same. There were no two ways of looking at it. She stared at their huge wingspans with envy, wondering if she'd be able to keep up. But, nervous though the thought made her, nothing could dim her excitement and she beat her wings valiantly, determined that neither of them should see her worry.

Wales! She explored the sound in her mind as they flew down lower through the first wispy strands of the cloud that blanketed Earth far below. She wondered what it would be like. She had never paid very much attention to planetary geography back in angel school, preferring the broader astronomical sweep of the Cosmos as a whole, and now had not the slightest idea where 'Wales' was. It sounded to her like it was maybe eastern European, perhaps near somewhere like Latvia or Estonia (she had heard of them). Or maybe it was one of the little African countries, near somewhere like Chad. Yes, that sounded possible, Chad, Burkina Faso... Wales. It was definitely Africa.

But the place Josh led them to didn't, to Raffie, look the way she thought Africa ought to at all. In fact, it didn't actually feel like anywhere she had ever previously imagined. They landed on what, Josh informed her, was the top of a large mountain. But she had to take his word for that, because it was so shrouded in fog that it was impossible to see. Even worse, a driving rain was falling and the ground underfoot was waterlogged and sodden.

A strange baaing sound echoed eerily through the mist as they touched down. 'Sheep,' said Josh briefly, in response to Raffie's amazed look. 'You know, little woolly creatures with four legs. Not very bright. That one's lost by the sound of it. Hang on!' He disappeared and returned seconds later with a huge beam on his face. 'It's all right,' he announced. 'It was a lamb that had got separated from its mother. I just took it back.'

Libertybel, who had been peering round with interest, said, 'So where's this cottage then? I thought we were supposed to be going straight to it.'

'Yes, we were.' Josh consulted the map that Flurripurel had given them with the instructions and said, 'No, there's no mistake. We're exactly where we're supposed to be, and the cottage ought to be just in front of us, over there...'

They all peered in the direction of his pointing hand, and he blew gently, parting the swirling fog. It rolled grudgingly back, and Raffie just made out, in a small hollow, what looked to be a disintegrating haystack, floating in a pond of evil-looking water. 'Gee,' said Libertybel. 'Is that it?'

'Uuum...' Josh frowned and stared again at the instructions, then said, 'I haven't a clue. If it is, it's still slightly out from where it's supposed to be, and Flurripurel describes it as...' he read from the paper, '... a charming little stone built, rustic cottage with slate roof, but in need of some refurbishment and without the benefit of fitted amenities.'

'Fitted what?' repeated Raffie.

She was totally lost. Josh and Libertybel exchanged glances. Libertybel said, 'He means things like no bathroom or plumbing.' Then, as Raffie looked even more bewildered, he explained, 'Flurry's pretty strange, because he was a human being once, you see. He was what they call an estate agent back on Earth, before he died and got made an angel. But he still insists on describing everything as if he's writing house details. Drizzle's warned him about it, because Flurry does have a tendency to exaggerate things and a few angels have got lost following his directions, but he won't change. Although,' he added, 'he does now include a disclaimer at the bottom of all instructions, saying he won't accept responsibility for accuracy.'

'Yes, well,' Josh looked annoyed. 'But does that mean that haystack thing is the cottage we've been sent to or not?' He flew forward, and the other two watched as he circled the heap from above, and then suddenly swooped, prodding and peering intently at the sides. 'No...' he called back. 'I don't think this is it. I think this really *is* hay, but it's floating. It's been washed away from somewhere.' He rejoined them and said with despair, 'It's the directions. They're definitely wrong. But that's really strange. Although Flurripurel exaggerates, I've never heard of him sending anyone to totally the wrong place before. The cottage must be somewhere here. Maybe there was a landslide, and everything got swept away.' He looked around worriedly and then muttered, 'There's nothing for it, we're going to have to spread out and search. Bel, you take the peak. I'll go downhill... and you have a good scout round here, Raffie.'

The two of them disappeared, and Raffie found herself all alone on the sodden slope. She looked around anxiously, completely at a loss what to do, and then began to glide cautiously back and forth across the hillside, peering intently this way and that. It was slowly dawning on her that this was definitely not Africa because it was far too wet and cold. But wherever it was, it was very strange, and there was something that felt almost hostile in the air. Another eerie baaing echoed forlornly across the hillside, and somewhere away over to the left she could hear the tinkling of a stream. But it was not a friendly sound, and she found herself wishing that Josh and Libertybel would return. Wherever they had gone, however, it seemed to be taking a long time, and she continued to skim backwards and forwards, all the time casting anxious looks back over her shoulder.

Silence. Below, beads of heavy moisture carpeted the scrubby grass and bushes like a shroud, while here and there the rocks that pushed intermittently through the ground glistened darkly: but of the cottage, there was no sign. And then, through the groping fingers of swirling fog, she caught a sudden glimpse of a tumbledown house.

It was not at all like she had imagined from Flurripurel's description. Rustic, yes, but charming? No, not by any stretch of the imagination. The squat building was grey and cramped-looking, with a skew-whiff door beneath a broken lintel, and two mean little windows crammed up either side, one with broken glass. It looked derelict, but through the smashed pane Raffie made out a feeble light. It seemed to flicker uncertainly, and then heave itself up onto the stone sill, before crawling weakly out into the clammy gloom.

'Gosh!' breathed Raffie. Unlikely as it looked, she knew immediately that she had found the missing cottage and, without thinking, zoomed across to it excitedly, ignoring her feelings of unease.

As she drew close, however, she felt as if a malign kind of tentacle were reaching out and winding itself around her wings, suffocating her and sending icy chills down her spine. Surprised, she stopped and beat back strongly with her wings, struggling to maintain some kind of distance. From the cottage came a low kind of moan, a peculiar sound that intensified the feeling of terror that seemed to rise up from the ground. Raffie had never felt anything like it before. It was like a kind of absence of life, dark and full of despair. She struggled back, landing heavily on the ground and scrabbling to get some kind of foothold on the boggy Earth. But it was no good, something irresistible seemed to be reaching out and drawing her towards it, sucking her in.

Clutching wildly at the slippery grass, Raffie began to slither and slide towards the cottage; ahead of her the ancient door, as if pulled back by an unseen hand, began to creak slowly open. The force grew stronger as she came closer and, with one last huge effort of hands and wings, she made a wild grab at the doorposts, bumping heavily against the rotting frame.

The surface crumbled beneath her touch, and her fingers locked onto the hard stone underneath. Panting, she tumbled onto the step and found herself staring straight into a tiny little room that looked as if it had not seen a duster, broom or human occupant in years. If the mess up in the Rain Room had been bad, then this, as the other angels had warned, was infinitely worse. Dust lay in thick, congealing ridges along the sides where the walls met the floor. Cobwebs hung across the corners of the room in heavy, dusty drapes, and everywhere there were untidy piles of books, papers and magazines – all heaped together higgledy-piggledy, brown and curling with age. Then, however, to her great surprise, Raffie became aware of two frail old people, sitting crouched with terror at the table that stood in the centre of all the mess. It too was littered with papers and dirty crockery, and perched in the middle of it was the rusty paraffin lamp whose feeble rays had first drawn her from outside.

'It's no good, Evan,' the old woman trembled, as Raffie took all this in. 'Nobody's going to come up here. The weather's still too bad.' Raffie had no problem understanding of course, because angels hear the meaning rather than language, and understand everyone and everything throughout the created world.

Now as if in agreement with the old woman's words, the cottage gave a loud creak, and then the posts Raffie was clutching shifted and seemed to slide. 'Oooh!' wailed the old man, reaching out and grabbing the base of the lamp just in time to stop it crashing to the floor. 'I tell you, Bethan, we've got to get out of here. The whole place is going to go down the mountain any minute! That must be a good metre in the last half hour!' He struggled in vain to rise, clutching at the wooden table for support, and Raffie saw two broken walking sticks lying at his side on the floor in a great puddle of water. As he shifted, she also caught a glimpse under the table of something dark and squat that seemed to hiss and pull back into the shadows as the light fell on it. She thought she saw a glint of teeth. Then such a terrible stench suddenly wafted into the air that the angel recoiled and began to cough violently.

'What was that?' asked the old woman, looking round.

She turned watery eyes towards the door, a hopeful expression lighting her lined old face, and exclaimed, 'Evan! It's lighter, I'm sure. I think the fog must be lifting – can't you feel it? If we can just get to the door…'

She too now struggled to rise to her feet, and the old man, following the direction of her eyes, glanced towards the door. For a moment Raffie had the oddest sensation that they were looking straight at her and she was filled with alarm, as it had been drummed into her that heavenly visitors were at all times to remain invisible, unless expressly told otherwise. Then, however, she realized that they were looking beyond her and out through the door, and that they could not actually make anything out, because of the murk and gloom outside. Relief flooded through her, but it was short-lived because the thing under the table, whatever it was, suddenly lunged forwards and swatted angrily at the old man's legs, so that he gave a despairing cry and crashed back down heavily onto the chair.

Abruptly, the pressure Raffie had been feeling ever since she first caught sight of the cottage eased, and she took advantage to shake herself and pull free. Then she whipped the lightning rod she had been issued with from her bag and pointed it with quivering fingers towards the table. The thing cowering underneath hissed and spat and tried in vain to hide itself, crouching away in the far corner behind the rickety legs, and Raffie found herself looking at quite one of the ugliest and most fearsome creatures she had ever seen.

It was not very big, but it was black and covered in a kind of horny, warty skin, while its bloodshot eyes, rolling drunkenly around the room, seemed to shoot venom at everything they saw. As the brilliant light from the rod fell on it, it spat violently and tried to withdraw further into the shadows.

'Evan,' cried the old woman again, hope thrilling through her voice, 'I'm sure we're going to be all right. Just hold on, won't you!'

In response the old man moaned, but Raffie ignored them. There was something terrible here, no question, and she knew that she had to get it away. Whatever might have happened to the cottage as a result of the storm, she knew that this horrible creature was the real cause of the problem. How long it could have been there, she had no idea, but she knew instinctively that it had somehow exploited the fury of the storm in order to grow in power, and now she could feel it feeding on the old people's dread. It was this that had been pulling her.

Holding the rod before her like a sword, Raffie slowly advanced into the room and peered cautiously beneath the table. The old woman's eyes seemed to follow her, a gleam of hope in their watery depths. She said wearily, 'Oh, I don't know, Evan. I think I must be imagining things.'

'Huum,' muttered Raffie. She poked down beneath the table and, with an explosion of fury, the small black creature erupted out into the centre of the room, spitting angrily and flailing at the air with dirt-encrusted talons.

Startled, Raffie gave a small scream and fell back, wondering what on Earth to do next. She found it even more horrid when she examined it closely; but she could also now see only too clearly that it was extremely annoyed. The black spiky ridge along its back stood up on end and the eyes, flashing around as it looked for a way of escape, gave off poisonous sparks. 'Move,' commanded Raffie, sounding a lot braver than she felt. She clutched the rod and moved further into the room, trying to manoeuvre the creature towards the door.

Immediately understanding her purpose, the monster whirled round and opened its jaws, sending a great blast of stinging, sulphurous air in Raffie's direction as it opened its mouth. 'In your dreams, angel!' it spat angrily. 'You're the one who's got to go! You don't have any call here. This hole, and these people, belong to me!'

Raffie glared at it, but she wasn't about to start a debate with this vile-looking thing. 'Get out!' she shrieked. 'What are you talking about? This place doesn't belong to you!' She stabbed at its back with the rod, and the creature danced away across the room in fury, then gathered itself in the far corner for attack.

'You've asked for this!' it howled back. 'You can't just come in here and start throwing your weight around! You may serve His High and Mightiness, but I've got rights, I have. *And* I've got the deeds of possession to prove it. These two signed everything over years ago.'

'Rubbish,' snapped back Raffie, not really having a clue what the beast was talking about, but feeling it was unwise to pursue the subject. 'I don't know what you're on about, but I'm sure you shouldn't be here like this, whatever these two might have signed. I wouldn't have been...'

Her last words ended in a small scream as the creature suddenly launched itself at her and fastened onto her arms, trying to knock the rod away from her grip. But, delicate though Raffie may have appeared, she was also very brave and, despite the pain, now she held on for dear life. So did the creature. Locked together, the two of them began to sway and tumble around the room in a bizarre kind of dance, each struggling to get a grip on the other.

Over at the table the old man groaned and said feebly, 'I don't feel at all well, Bethan. I feel as if I've come over all queer.'

'Hush,' said the old woman fixedly. Raffie turned her head and found the old woman's eyes once again turned pleadingly towards her. 'Whoever, or whatever you are,' the woman breathed, '... if you're there at all... Please help us.'

Raffie had been feeling close to collapse, unable to resist the strength in the creature's leathery arms, but the old woman's words now acted as a spur. It was enough. The angel felt a thin trickle of strength pulse through her frame, and with a tremendous effort of will she gathered herself together and thrust the foul creature away. Just then, there was a piercing cry from over by the door, and she looked up in time to see Josh and Libertybel catapult in through the frame, exploding into the room with a blaze of light. They surged forwards and grabbed hold of the thing by each arm, wrestling it back and away.

The creature, whatever it was, put up a terrible fight, but it was no match for the three young angels. Raffie sank weakly to the floor as they at last managed to pin it up against the wall and tied its claws with some thin rope that Libertybel snatched from the bottom of his bag. 'It isn't much,' he said, standing back, panting, 'but I think it'll hold until we get some of the Watchers down here to deal with it.'

Raffie tottered to her feet, eyeing the beast with distaste. Her head was swimming, and for some reason she was finding it difficult to breathe. Angels can't die in the same way humans can, of course, but they can be hurt and their spirits can become so weakened that their forms dissolve so that they cease to exist as individuals at all.

'What is it?' she demanded weakly, panting and clutching at the table for support. 'I could feel it sucking me towards it the moment I saw the cottage, and then, when I got here and tried to get it out into the light, it attacked me.'

Securing a last knot, Josh looked round and said, 'It's an imp. A kind of very junior demon… in training, just like we are. But I had no idea there was something like this down here, and I suspect that Drizzlewobbel hadn't either, because there's no way we'd have been sent here on our own to deal with something like this.'

The imp, firmly gagged though it now was, made a gurgling sound and joggled up and down furiously. Raffie jumped and stepped back. Libertybel looked grim, but he paused to pat her on the back and said, 'Hey, you did well, you know! But what possessed you to try to take it on by yourself?'

Raffie felt really strange. 'I… I didn't have much choice,' she grimaced. 'Like I said… I tried to get it out into the light to see what it was, and it attacked me. But they helped…' A strange kind of giddiness stole over her, but she managed to nod towards the old couple, and Josh and Libertybel, becoming aware of them for the first time, both turned and stared. But to Raffie's astonishment an amazing transformation seemed to have come over the pair. The old man was smiling and had managed to struggle to his feet, while his wife was already lurching her way to the door. 'Come on, Evan,' she panted excitedly. 'It's definitely brighter now. Let's take the chance and go and get help.'

Libertybel stared after them, and then threw a quick glance towards Raffie. 'So what shall we do now?' he snapped, addressing himself to Josh. He sounded worried, and Raffie looked at him, puzzled. She was having some difficulty concentrating, but all the same she couldn't quite make out why he should be fussing – after all, the imp was tied up. There couldn't be any danger now.

But Josh was looking worried as well. He too glanced at her and then said bleakly, 'I'm not sure. Could you go with the old couple, Bel, and get them down to safety? I'll take Raffie back and report to Flurripurel. And we'll get some Watchers down here.'

Raffie stared at him indignantly. There was something about his tone that she didn't quite like. She felt that he was talking to Libertybel as if she weren't there, or didn't matter somehow, and she felt insulted. She might be new, she thought furiously, but how dared the two of them act as if they were the only ones that mattered? After all, who had it been who had found the cottage in the first place?

She opened her mouth to protest, and found Josh staring at her unhappily. 'Do you think you're going to be able to make it?' he asked.

She gaped. 'What?' she demanded. 'Of course. Why shouldn't I?'

'Well, with that!'

Libertybel pointed to her arm and, puzzled, Raffie

looked down to find a long gaping tear; there also seemed to be a chunk missing from one of her wings. Just then, as if it had only been waiting for the chance of recognition, a searing pain shot up her left side. 'Ooh,' she said, shivering. She suddenly felt distinctly peculiar.

Bel turned back to Josh. 'Are you sure you can get her back, buddy?'

Josh looked gloomy but nodded. 'Yes,' he said. 'Besides, we can't leave those two on their own. Who knows what else might be hanging around out there?'

'There was nothing indicated in the orders.'

'I know, but neither was this thing.'

The two angels stared at each other grimly, and Raffie thought that she detected some sort of communication pass between them. But she couldn't really understand it, and she felt just too weary to pursue the matter.

'OK,' said Bel. 'If you're sure?'

Josh nodded, and Bel half smiled and then turned and nodded towards Raffie. 'So long, kid,' he said briefly. 'Don't worry, you're going to make it.' Then, without a backwards glance, he spun round and shot out through the door after the two old people, who were now stumbling and sliding their way down the muddy slope.

Josh watched him for a moment, a bleak expression on his face, and then began to rummage in his bag. Seeing the movement, the imp on the floor wriggled and tried to lunge at his feet. The angel sidestepped and then pushed it roughly back against the wall. 'Stay!' he snapped. He brought out a small flask and held it towards Raffie. 'Here,' he commanded. 'Have a drink of this. It'll make you feel a bit better.'

Now unable to make any kind of decision for herself, Raffie took it obediently, wondering what it was. She discovered it had a strange kind of fragrance, light and filled with all kinds of pungent aromas that reminded her of the sun-drenched hills and rippling streams that she knew so well up in the heavens. And then, as it slid over her tongue, a kind of fire seemed to explode in her mouth and she choked. 'Yes,' remarked Josh. He sounded pleased. 'It does have that effect. It's strong stuff, but drink it down… it'll get you back.'

Raffie wanted to ask why she should *need* anything to get her back. She couldn't make head nor tail of any of this. She had no chance, however, because Josh abruptly launched off into the air, calling back over his shoulder, 'Try to keep up… And if you feel you can't, grab hold of me!'

Aware at last of a need for urgency, Raffie cast one last look at the imp still wriggling on the floor and then flung herself into the air after Josh. There was no way she wanted to stay behind with that thing! But it was all most peculiar. She really did feel odd, almost as if she wasn't quite there; her arm was really hurting now, while her wings felt like lead.

They hurtled up through the heavens, Raffie struggling to keep up, the tips of her wings going numb. But, though she did her very best, the feeling of unreality that had been creeping up on her ever since the fight seemed to increase the higher they flew. It was all so bizarre. She felt so tired, and the stars above seemed to be spinning in long, great… curving… loops… Not knowing what she was doing, she slid sideways and down, wings sagging, and then suddenly jolted back to alertness as hands inserted themselves roughly under her arms. Surprised, she opened her eyes, and Josh's face swam hazily into focus. 'Come on, Raffie,' he said urgently. 'Don't give up on me now. It's not far. We're almost there.'

Then they were again beating their way upwards, and Raffie felt herself being pulled along like an unwieldy sack of potatoes. She wasn't really sure what happened after that, although she had a hazy recollection later that Josh had carried her, and she knew that he had been talking to her, trying to keep her awake, although she couldn't remember what he'd said. But she knew that she had felt guilty because, all the time he was bearing her upwards, she could feel that he was weakening too, only she didn't have any strength to help. And then she had slipped wearily into a pit of shimmering darkness, where vivid dreams had seemed to leap out at her and fingers had jabbed through frightening clouds of mist, clawing her back. But of what actually happened as she and Josh sped through the heavens, she had no memory at all.

When she awoke later, it was to find Lucis bending over her, a worried frown on his face, and she wasn't sure at first whether she was still dreaming or not. 'Hello,' she croaked, surprised to discover her mouth felt so dry.

'Hello,' replied Lucis gently. 'Back with us at last, Raffie. How are you feeling now?'

Raffie stared up at him, astonished by his concern. There was a dull pain in her right arm, and she felt a bit odd still, but she didn't think there was anything to fuss about. 'OK, I think,' she said cautiously, struggling to sit up. 'Why?'

She became aware of another angel hovering behind

him, and was surprised to see it was one of the Guardians. 'She'll be all right now,' said that grand being reassuringly. 'No need to worry. You got her back in time, Joshuel.'

Raffie noticed that Josh was standing beside her, his face ashen. 'What's the matter?' she demanded, now seriously worried, and struggling even harder to pull herself upright. 'Where am I?'

Lucis looked stern, but he inserted an arm under her wings and helped her gently up into a sitting position. 'You gave us all quite a scare, you know, Raffie,' he said. 'You're up in a hospital wing of one of the first level Mansions. Joshuel brought you, and there was a time back there when we thought we'd lost you. The Guardian took care of you.'

Raffie was almost too astonished for words. 'But why?' she asked. 'What happened?'

The Guardian now stepped forward. 'Do you remember anything at all?' she asked gently.

Raffie stared at her. She felt unnerved to be that close to so exalted an angel as one of the Guardians. She had only ever before seen one in the distance, when he had visited the school just before she had been assigned to active training with Lucis. Guardians, like the Cherubs and Seraphs, were among the highest ranking of angels and, as their name implied, their function was to care for the welfare of all created things – which included other angels. 'I … I think so,' she stammered. 'I'm not sure… I remember the cottage down in Wales. And I remember a horrible beast… an imp.'

'Do you remember it wounding you?'

Raffie shook her head. 'Not really,' she whispered.

'Although later…'

She trailed off, and the Guardian very lightly touched her arm. 'It bit you,' she explained softly. 'Demon venom had got into your blood. That imp you took on was almost fully grown. You were infected and the poison was eating into your system. If Joshuel hadn't got you back so promptly, you'd have been destroyed. Your form would have melted away.'

'Wow!' said Raffie. She couldn't think of anything else to say.

She turned and stared at Josh, who went crimson and nodded. 'It's true,' he confirmed. 'Bel and I noticed there was something wrong the moment we came in and saw the imp, but we didn't realize how bad it was until we saw the bites on your arm and wing. And then we didn't want to worry you.'

'Yes,' said Lucis seriously, 'you've been very lucky. What possessed you to try to take on a full-grown imp by yourself, Raffie? Why didn't you call for assistance?'

She flushed. 'I didn't realize what it was.' She bit her lip. 'I just wanted to help, that was all. And I didn't really have much choice at the time. It just sort of sucked me in and then went for me.'

The Guardian nodded her head sagely. 'Yes,' she said, 'that's the way with those horrible creatures. We often don't know they're there till it's too late. But you really should have tried to go and get help. As I understand it, it was you who first stirred the thing up by prodding it. And Joshuel tells me that you hadn't even taken any kind of precautions.'

'But I didn't know you had to!' blurted out Raffie,

wanting desperately to justify herself. 'And I didn't know what it was. Honestly! All I could see was that it was hurting those two old people down there, and that it wouldn't let them go. I was only trying to help.'

Lucis looked across at the Guardian, and they exchanged a sigh. 'I did tell you,' he said despairingly. 'This young angel is a magnet for trouble! Always acts before she thinks, but her intentions are good. The trouble was, nobody knew there was an imp down there.'

'Yes,' broke in Josh excitedly. 'It really wasn't her fault, Guardian, honestly. Any one of us would have done exactly the same. That thing attacked her, but she put up a tremendous fight... and she really did save those two old people. The imp had made the cottage begin to slide down the mountain, and it wasn't allowing them to get out. Any longer and it would have destroyed them completely, and then they'd have been totally lost to us forever, because the Enemy had cut them off years ago and they'd lacked any kind of will to find a way back. It was only because they were in so much trouble that they began to struggle at all, and Raffie heard and flew to their aid and...'

'Yes, yes, I know.' The Guardian held up a hand, silencing him. 'But that doesn't alter the fact that all you young angels know perfectly well that there are procedures for dealing with this sort of thing... and I hope for the future that all three of you will understand why. The minute Raffie felt that pull, she should have come and got Lucis here. He would have dealt with it immediately, and without any of this trouble.'

'Oh come, Guardian.' Lucis now also made a move to protest. 'Joshuel is quite right. Raffael did try to help, and it's true that she had never seen an imp before… and this *was* a particularly nasty one. It gave some trouble even when I went down there.'

'What?' interrupted Raffie, her eyes round. 'What do you mean? Did you go down there, Lucis?'

'*Did* he,' broke in Josh, unable any longer to contain himself. 'You should have seen him, Raffie! He flew down in such a rage after I'd brought you in, and he burst into the cottage with a blaze of the most tremendous light. The imp had got free by then, and it had called some of its chums in, and they were waiting for him. Bel and I were just behind, because we wanted to see what happened, and the Guardian had said we could go, as long as we kept out of the way. And Lucis drew his sword and he just flew straight at them. It was terrific! There was the most awful struggle and…'

'Yes, well,' said Lucis hastily, 'I don't think we need to relive the whole thing again now, Joshuel. Suffice to say, all three of the little tykes have now been dealt with, and none of them will cause trouble any more.'

The Guardian raised an eyebrow. 'Did you throw them into the pit?' she asked.

'Yes,' Lucis nodded. 'They won't get out of there again in a hurry.' He turned back to Raffie. 'But the point is, you should not have tackled it on your own. You're right at the start of your training, Raffael, and you haven't had any kind of preparation for this sort of thing yet. Neither, of course, have Joshuel or Libertybel. Students aren't supposed to meet imps or demons until they're at least third level and have undergone elementary combat training, and then only under supervision. All of you have been very, very lucky.'

'Quite right,' agreed the Guardian. 'But,' she smiled, 'that doesn't mean that you didn't all do very well in the circumstances. You coped with a difficult situation and brought it to our attention, and it has all been dealt with now. However, I think all three of you can go to an easier placing for a while, to give you all a chance to recover.'

'Oh, but…!'

Josh looked as if he was about to protest, but she quelled him with a glance. 'I shall speak to Head of Assignments immediately,' she said firmly, 'and we'll see if we can come up with something a little less demanding.'

5
A Bit of a Handful

Madame Germinel fluffed out the magnificent feathers of her upper wings and said plaintively, 'Oh, là, là! What am I supposed to do with the three of you? We are fully staffed at the moment.'

Josh, Bel and Raffie exchanged looks. The Guardian had gone through a whole list of departments, rejecting them all as far too potentially dangerous, and had finally settled on 'BABE'. 'Bioluminescent And Biological Embryos,' she had explained with a sigh, 'BABE for short. It's mainly transporting ensouled, pre-birth humans down to their mothers at the moment of conception, and overseeing implantation into the womb. I would hope that even you three couldn't get into trouble with that.'

But Madame Germinel was not at all pleased at the prospect of having to find employment for three completely inexperienced students. 'We are a 'ighly specialized department,' she complained bitterly. 'And I just wish that the Guardian would stop looking on us as some kind of soft option. The placing of new souls is 'ighly skilled and demands absolute precision of matching. His Majesty is very thorough about this sort of thing. He plans right down to the last detail, and we 'ave to make absolutely sure his wishes are carried out. There are all sorts of things we 'ave to take into account.' Then she added, 'And all sorts of things that can go wrong.

Many of our angels come under the most enormous attack.'

Bel brightened visibly. Josh cleared his throat and said hastily, 'I'm sure we can do it, ma'am. It's true that none of us has done this sort of thing before, but we're all very eager to learn, and we can all follow instructions.'

Madame Germinel looked at his huge frame and sighed. 'Yes,' she agreed, 'I am sure you will try, but let me put it this way… Our operatives are usually somewhat – 'ow can I say this – less strapping in appearance. You two at least,' she gestured towards Libertybel as well, 'look as if you might be more at 'ome doing Watcher duty out on the perimeters of the Universe. Although I must say,' she added, looking measuringly at Raffie, 'you at least, my dear, have more of the appearance of the angelic messenger.' She glanced down at the report in her hand, frowned and said, 'Although it says 'ere that it is you who were "initially responsible for the engagement of hostilities" down on Earth, and that you were wounded. Where exactly was that, by the way?' she demanded, peering up over the narrow rims of the glasses perched on the end of her long and rather elegant nose.

'Wales,' replied Raffie immediately. The expression on the archangel's face told her that this was the wrong reply, and she blushed and muttered, 'Sorry, on my right arm and wing.'

Madame Germinel's expression softened. 'Oh yes, yes, I can see,' she clucked, stooping and pushing the glasses further up her nose to see better. 'And how are you now? 'Ealing well?'

'Yes, thank you.'

'Good.' Madame Germinel paused, staring at the fading scar, and then sighed, 'A nasty business all round really... but I am told you three actually performed rather well, so we shall see. Aureyel!' She turned to a slender-looking, mid-ranking angel just coming in through the massed banks of cloud that led into the department, and said, 'Take Raffael, Joshuel and Libertybel and show them around the station. And then take them down to the nurseries and fill them in on their duties.'

Aureyel nodded, a huge and rather inane smile pinned to his face, and said, 'Of course, madame. I'd be delighted.' Josh and Bel stared at each other, and a look passed between them – a look that said, told you so, and get me out of this, quick.

They had not been at all pleased when they had first learned where they were to be assigned. 'It's totally girly,' Bel said, disgusted. 'The only thing that could possibly be worse would be for them to have given us harps and say we all had to have singing lessons!'

Josh laughed and said, 'No danger of that. I've heard your voice!'

But Raffie was puzzled. She had never heard of BABE before, and couldn't understand why the other two looked so glum. Josh soon filled her in. 'You never see any kind of action there,' he explained. 'All you do is look after pre-birth humans, and then take them down as soon as they're conceived. And all the angels who choose to go there are sort of airy-fairy and a bit naff.'

'Yeah,' echoed Bel. 'It's a known fact that it's only the angels who are really soft, or totally useless at anything else, who end up there!'

Raffie had thought that they were being rather harsh, but now, looking at Aureyel, she decided that maybe they had been right. Madame Germinel might be a bit fierce, but Aureyel looked the kind of angel who wouldn't know his Milky Way from his aurora borealis, and Raffie's spirits sank. She felt it was going to be rather boring being assigned to BABE.

They did a quick tour of the station, which, as far as Raffie could see, was mostly made up of nurseries and some rather strange-looking laboratories, where white-robed angels flitted this way and that and appeared to be doing nothing very much – but doing it very busily. Then at last they came to a small shaded room, where soft music was playing and the lights were dimmed. 'This is where we look after pre-birth damaged souls,' explained Aureyel, his voice hushed, nodding towards one of the workers, who smiled radiantly. 'They've usually been injured during transfer, and had to be brought back for healing and reassignment. Although sometimes too,' he whispered, dropping his voice even more and looking round quickly to make sure they were not overheard, 'when His Majesty has lined one of them up for a particularly important job down on Earth, somehow the Enemy gets wind of it and tries to interfere before they're safely down. You wouldn't believe some of the attacks I've seen. I tell you, there can be real battles!' He shook his head and muttered, 'And it's not been unknown for us to lose a few too.'

Dire though this sounded, Bel brightened visibly and winked over at Josh. But Aureyel glowered reprovingly and hissed, 'No, I can assure you, it's very far from being fun.

The whole department is subject to almost constant attack. Were it not for the fact that we are cloaked by an invisibility curtain, which means that the Enemy and his forces find it very difficult to see us – and that the Watchers keep a patrol on our boundaries – we would be in a state of constant war.'

But Aureyel was apparently becoming bored, because he glanced round and said impatiently, 'But we need to get a move on. I'm under strict instructions to take you down to Nursery Level 3, and if we're not there before you're due for assignment there'll be trouble.'

He set off rapidly towards the door. Josh and Bel immediately abandoned their inspection of a control panel they'd found, and fell in behind. Raffie, however, stayed a moment longer, gazing round. She was puzzled. She hadn't realized that being human and birth could be so hazardous, and all sorts of questions were bubbling in her mind. But Aureyel was disappearing and, fearful of being left, she took to her wings and set off in pursuit.

'So what are we going to be doing then?' demanded Josh, as they followed hot on the angel's heels.

'Transfer duty,' flung back Aureyel briefly. There was an air of anxiety in his manner now, and he looked as if he didn't want to delay. 'Do hurry up,' he urged. 'Madame Germinel said I wasn't to let you waste time. You've been assigned to Dispatch, I believe, which means you're going to be carrying humans down to Earth and helping them settle in.'

Aureyel almost ran through the last level, and they arrived panting in a huge hall that bore the legend 'Pickup Point – Level 3' over the cloud-wrapped entrance.

If the levels above had been quiet, this one more than made up for it. It was full of roped-off sections and large pens that stood end to end and were all crammed with small babies. Unlike on Earth, however, these babies walked around and talked, some extremely loudly; quite a few seemed to be jostling and shoving each other, and every once in a while a noisy argument seemed to erupt. 'They're due for transfer any moment,' explained Aureyel, catching his breath, and looking around distractedly. 'You'll notice that they've all already been clothed in the bodies that they'll grow into in the womb and use for the rest of their lives on Earth. But unfortunately we can't clothe them without also giving them the beginnings of their future terrestrial personalities, which is why they're having these arguments all over the place. It can be very wearing.'

He worked out where they were supposed to go, and led the way over to a long line of angels standing about halfway down the hall, quietly waiting to receive their various charges. To Raffie it seemed that there was a huge number of them and no sooner had they received their individual assignments and flown off than it seemed their places were taken by a dozen more.

At the head of the queue stood a very impressive-looking angel, clutching a long scroll that was unfurling itself untidily onto the floor. As each baby came up, she consulted the scroll closely and then handed the child to the next angel waiting in line, saying things like, 'Liverpool Maternity Hospital, England, UK. Delivery Suite E... Fourth house on the left, Nanouk's inuit settlement, the North Pole.'

It was like a conveyor belt and Raffie felt her eyes goggle. She had never seen so many babies before. Indeed, she had never imagined that so many could exist, not all at the same time and in the same place – even given the fact of eternity. But Aureyel was speaking again, and she shook her head, trying to pay attention.

'... All you've got to do,' the angel was saying, 'is make sure that you get the right baby to the right mother, and if you pay attention to the name tags you can't go wrong. So if you'd just like to get in line over there and wait your turn, you can be off on your first assignments as soon as possible.'

Duty done, Aureyel floated away and Josh, Libertybel and Raffie joined the queue. Bel looked mutinous. 'Honestly,' he muttered, 'I never thought I'd end up doing this. This is nanny duty!'

'But you heard what Aureyel said,' muttered back Josh. 'Protecting angels have to guard assigned humans, and they're constantly under attack. I think this could actually be fun.'

'Huh!' replied Bel.

The queue seemed to move with amazing speed, and they quickly found themselves almost at the head. As it came to Bel's turn, he moved forward and glumly held out his arms, as they had seen all the others do, and a small human with a shock of black hair was deposited none too gently in his outstretched fists. 'Mongolia,' intoned the supervising angel. 'Fifth house from the westerly junction of the main street running through Tsomog.'

The baby reached out a hand and biffed Bel on the nose, and he grimaced. 'There you are,' said Josh behind.

'What did Aureyel tell us? Constant battle!'

'Next!' said the supervising angel.

Bel cast on him a look that spoke volumes and flew off, a sour expression on his face. In his arms the child wriggled determinedly. Josh and Raffie heard Bel's voice float back, 'Ouch! That hurt. Just quit that, will you!'

'Arms!' snapped a voice.

Raffie, standing next in line, jumped. 'Sorry?' she asked, blinking.

The supervising angel stared at her. 'Arms,' she repeated. 'Hold them out, please.'

Josh, standing just behind, sniggered. He seemed to be finding the whole thing enormously funny. Raffie flushed with irritation but obediently held out her arms, and then almost fainted with horror as eight tiny bundles were thrust towards her. 'Just stand still, please,' commanded the supervising angel. 'This is only half your consignment.'

'Half?' repeated Raffie, stunned. 'But it can't be! I mean… I thought babies usually came in ones.'

'Or twos,' remarked Josh helpfully from behind. 'They're called twins, you know.'

Raffie ignored him. 'Surely there's a mistake?'

'No mistake,' the supervising angel said frostily. She was clearly not used to having her instructions questioned.

'Please check,' said Raffie desperately.

The supervising angel stared at her, then sighed and glanced down at the manifest in her hands. 'No,' she said wearily. 'Just as I told you. Sixteen. Special delivery. Hold still, please, or you'll drop them.'

Raffie felt herself grow hot. 'But I can't possibly manage sixteen,' she protested. 'I can hardly even hold these eight. They won't keep still.'

But the supervising angel didn't seem to be paying any attention. She merely gathered together another eight, quickly checking the labels, and then tried to load them too into Raffie's arms. It was a disaster. Small children tumbled all over the floor. 'For heaven's sake!' snapped the supervising angel, clearly annoyed.

'I told you!' retorted Raffie. 'There are too many of them. I can't possibly manage sixteen all in one go. Babies don't come in these kinds of numbers. You must have got your list wrong!'

The supervising angel sighed heavily. It was a sigh that she seemed to have dragged up from somewhere deep within her angelic boots and which seemed to hold all the disillusioned gloom of her wrongly questioned world. She stared down at the babies, now scattering delightedly in all directions, raised her eyes to the higher heavens, as if declining all further responsibility for such unwarrantable chaos, and then very ostentatiously once again consulted the manifest in her hand. 'No,' she repeated, 'no mistake. There are definitely sixteen of them.' And then, relenting slightly, she added, 'It's a special IVF consignment, you see.'

'So what's that?' enquired Josh casually from behind, trying to detach one of the babies from the nearest celestial exit door, where it had climbed up and now seemed in imminent danger of floating off into space. 'Intrusive Vertical Fatalities? Impossibly Vexing Fledglings? What does it mean?'

The supervising angel looked surprised. 'IVF? Don't you know?'

Josh shook his head. 'Never heard of it.'

The supervising angel looked pained. 'It's a new technique the humans have developed,' she explained. 'Completely without divine authorization, but there you go. Their scientists take about twenty or thirty eggs, fertilize them in a test tube in a laboratory, and then re-implant the ones they select back into the mother. These –' she looked down at her list '– are all to go to the IVF Clinic, Santo Spiritu Hospital, Rome, Italy – although of course they won't all get used. But that's not my responsibility. They've been created now, and so they've got to go down. It's an absolute nightmare for us, of course,' she added, scooping up two more babies as they tried to sneak past her and shoving them back into Raffie's arms. 'Since they started all this, the paperwork we've had to do has quadrupled. You've no idea of the records we have to keep, and it's not helped at all when there are two or three possible couples all using the same batch. It's getting so as it's almost impossible to classify the parents these days! But the most important thing is to make absolutely sure that you do get each human into the right dish. The last thing we want is for an orangutan to end up with a human.'

Raffie could have cried. She was now clutching four babies, while angels behind her in the queue ran about trying furiously to round up the remaining twelve. 'But I can't carry all of them,' she protested again. 'There are far too many.'

The babies stared up at her with interest, and one raised its hand and gave a tug at her hair. 'Ouch!' said Raffie.

Two more babies were thrust towards her, one a great strapping child, with curly brown hair and a hostile expression, and the other a tiny little waif-like creature, with huge eyes and a few wisps of ash blond hair, who looked as if ambrosia (which angels are rather fond of) wouldn't melt in its mouth. It stared up at her solemnly, its expression impossible to read. Josh came up, clasping the other ten babies by hands, feet and any thing else he could get a grip on. 'Got them all now, I think!' he panted. 'But they're putting up a bit of a fight, and a couple of them have blacked each other's eyes. I think Raffie is right. She's never going to be able to manage all of them on her own.' He smiled angelically – as only angels really can, of course – and said, 'Would you like me to help her?'

6
The Problems of Science!

In the end it was settled that Josh would accompany Raffie down to the laboratory, and that they should carry eight babies each. Even this was almost too much, but the supervising angel had been adamant. The babies had been ordered for only one mother; therefore technically only one angel should be assigned to make delivery, and it mattered not whether there was one baby, or one hundred. The supervising angel had only finally agreed to the two of them going when it had been pointed out to her by Aureyel, who had come back over to investigate what all the fuss was about, that it was the first mission for both of them and, since it was clearly so complicated, it might be sensible to allow them to support each other.

When the supervisor had grudgingly agreed, Aureyel had drawn Josh and Raffie aside and said worriedly, 'I ought to warn you, there'll be a lot of Enemy activity down there. Enemy agents always lurk around these laboratories because there's so much potential to cause harm. The foetuses are very exposed, you see, not being safely tucked up inside a mother. So be very careful. You'll both be screened of course, which means though you can see each other you'll be invisible to the Enemy, and with a bit of luck they won't know you're there until it's too late. But don't imagine they won't be waiting for you. Imps and demons jump at the chance of getting their claws into humans before they've been born, and with sixteen of them it'll be all too easy for them to pick up on your presence and for you to lose a few.'

'What exactly do you think he meant?' Raffie asked later, as she and Josh winged their way down through the firmament towards Earth. 'Do you think we really are going to find demons down there? Will they attack us?'

Beside her, Josh shrugged. 'Who can say?' he shouted back. 'Sounded a bit hairy, but I don't think there'll be a problem. Remember, Aureyel said we'd be screened the whole time, so provided we're careful they shouldn't even realize we're there.' He grinned at her reassuringly and added, 'And anyway, even though we probably won't see them, if it's that much of a hotspot, there are bound to be Watchers around. They're always on the lookout for this sort of thing.'

Raffie bit her lip. She wasn't really very sure about all this warfare business. Wales had been a bit of a shock, and the Guardian, when she had assigned them, had said that Deliveries was safe, and yet now they were being warned to be on their guard. She wondered if everywhere on Earth was this dangerous, and wondered whether Lucis might be down there too. She knew very little of her mentor's work when he wasn't tutoring her. He would appear, literally, from out of the blue in order, as he put it, to check up on how she was getting on – and then promptly disappear. She had always vaguely assumed, when he turned up like that, that he had flown in from a long way away. She remembered one time when he had arrived looking distinctly ruffled. She had asked him then what it was he actually did, and he had replied evasively,

'Oh, this and that! You know… guard duty mainly.' She had thought at the time that he simply meant that he stood around keeping an eye on things. But now, as they flew down through the cloudy skies, she began to wonder if his work actually wasn't something rather more dangerous.

'Did you notice we had a storm warning over the Alps and northern Italy?' called Josh, breaking suddenly into her thoughts. 'Weather said to expect turbulence.' As if to confirm his words, a huge blast of warm air suddenly billowed up through the massed clouds, rocketing them aside as if they were no more than a couple of pieces of fluff. Raffie felt herself plunging down, sucked into a kind of thermal vortex. 'Watch yourself!' shouted Josh, diving after her.

She stabilized herself frantically with her wings, thrusting upwards, and pulled hard out of the current. One of the babies began to cry, and another – a little girl – wrapped its arms around her neck, almost strangling her. 'Hang on!' she shouted to them. 'Just a little bit of turbulence, that's all. Make sure you're strapped down.' The babies all checked the restraining harnesses that Aureyel had insisted they wear and Raffie flew on, acutely conscious of their eyes locked anxiously on her face.

'Are we going to be all right?' called one of the babies.

Raffie smiled reassuringly. 'Of course we are,' she said firmly. 'I've never lost a delivery yet!'

Josh battled his way to her side and grinned. 'Guess this is still the aftermath of your handiwork,' he called cheerfully. 'Bit rough though, isn't it!'

They flew on, buffeted and tossed by conflicting streams of air. Every once in a while, two opposing currents would clash against each other violently and there would be a huge clap of thunder that seemed to reverberate off the mountain tops now visible far below. 'Switzerland down there,' called Josh, pointing. 'Don't worry, always gets a bit rough over here. It's the Alps…' They ricocheted down another hundred metres and flew straight into the middle of what felt to be a wall of stinging rain. Being angels, the water didn't have much impact on Raffie or Josh of course, but the babies, who were already clothed in their human forms, all started to shriek. Josh began to sing loudly, a rather discordant song that he said was called a 'nursery rhyme', and the babies howled even louder. Raffie stared at him in despair. She would be very glad when this assignment was over.

As they flew out over the plains that fell away to the south of the Alps, however, the weather began to change. It began to feel warmer, and the clouds started to clear. Soon they found themselves flying out into brilliant sun. 'You can relax your harnesses now,' called Raffie to the still terrified children. 'I think we're through the worst bit. Plain flying now down to Rome!'

They swooped down, coming in low over Florence, and shot on with arrow-like precision towards the outlying hills of the capital. Beside her, Raffie could hear Josh talking merrily to the babies. 'We shall shortly be landing at Santo Spiritu,' he was yelling. 'Weather conditions are very pleasant down there and local time at the moment is three minutes past four. I hope you had a pleasant flight, and would like to thank you for choosing to fly…'

'We didn't,' interrupted one of the babies rudely. 'I'd have been quite happy to stay where we were, thank you.'

'Well, you might find yourself back in a couple of hours,' snapped back one of the others. A noisy argument erupted between them, and Josh threw Raffie a resigned glance. 'Not easy, are they?' he mouthed.

They discovered the clinic right at the centre of the vast, sprawling city now opening out beneath them in a haze of smoggy heat. As they approached, Josh consulted the map they had been given and then pointed to a particularly crowded hill a couple of miles ahead and said, 'Over there. It's that funny building with the square in front of it and the dome on top.'

Raffie looked to where he was pointing and gulped, totally unprepared for the sight that now met her eyes. Aureyel had been quite right, she realized, about possible Enemy activity. There were forces camped all round the building. Scarlet and green demons, dusty-looking grey imps, and some large warlike black angels with ugly faces and swords that glinted evilly in the sun. 'Don't worry,' called Josh, seeing Raffie's startled expression. 'We're screened, remember. With a bit of luck, we'll be in and out before they know. And seeing that lot, I'm absolutely positive there'll be Watchers around!'

Raffie shook her head. 'Hope you're right,' she yelled back. 'When Aureyel said there would be some Enemy activity, I wasn't exactly expecting this lot! Why are there so many?'

'What is it?' anxiously asked the baby girl, whose arms were still twined resolutely round Raffie's neck. 'What's wrong? Is there something there that shouldn't be?'

'No, of course not,' said Raffie immediately. 'It's fine.' She examined the baby girl closely and said cheerfully, hoping to divert her, 'So what's your name then?'

'Holly,' said the baby.

'That's pretty.'

But there was no time for further conversation. The two angels swooped down lower, hovering in the centre of the large square as they searched for an entrance. Raffie shivered. She felt she could almost see dark tentacles thrown out by the Enemy reaching towards them, searching and cold, probing at the air. 'Oh, I don't like it,' said Holly. She struggled to get away, and Raffie clamped her more firmly to her front. But Holly's fear infected the others, and they all now began to wail and cry, some of them clawing frantically in an effort to get away. Josh, she saw, was having similar difficulties. He looked up, red-faced, and said, 'Let's get inside. I don't think I'm going to be able to hang onto this lot much longer. And if they get away, that's it! They'll become visible and our cover will be blown!'

Raffie discovered that it was not easy flying with eight wilful and struggling babies, all intent on causing as much disruption as possible. Matters were not helped at all when one of them accidentally knocked her halo over her eyes. 'Oouf!' said Raffie, bumping and catapulting through a pillar she hadn't noticed, so that she narrowly missed an Enemy guard. 'Look, stop that, will you? I've already said, there's nothing to worry about, and we'll be inside in a minute.'

But it was easier said than done. The hospital before which they were standing seemed to have doors everywhere, and it was not immediately apparent where Josh and Raffie should go. 'Over here maybe!' called Josh, thrusting his way towards a pair of huge windows, shrouded against the glare of the late afternoon sun by a pair of heavy wooden shutters. 'If I've got the directions right, the laboratory should be just down the corridor that lies on the far side of this room.'

They flitted in, and Raffie felt a surge of horror as they narrowly missed flying straight into the arms of a huge sour-looking angel standing guard in the room just beyond. His face was dark, and he wore black, silver-edged robes that seemed to flash menacingly. As they shot past he frowned and stared around, and Raffie had the unpleasant feeling that he could sense something there. But though his eyes raked back and forth, he didn't stir, and with a feeling of wonderment Raffie slid past, close behind Josh. They found themselves standing in a long gloomy hall, with doors leading off and dark forbidding portraits lining the walls in between. The atmosphere felt dead. Raffie cringed and said, 'Are you sure we're in the right place?'

'Think so,' said Josh uncertainly, once again consulting the map. 'Yes, according to this, the laboratory is…' He raised a finger, swirling round and peering into the shadows, and then stopped, jabbing it towards a closed door over on the right. 'There!'

Raffie stared at it. It was painted a dull cream and looked unwelcoming and heavy, not at all the sort of place she would have associated with a happy event like birth. 'Gosh,' she breathed, 'looks a bit grim, doesn't it?'

Josh pulled a face, but set off determinedly towards the door. 'Grim or not,' he remarked, 'let's get this lot safely delivered and get out of here.' He shimmered and then disappeared through the wooden panels of the door, leaving a faint glow in his wake. But as Raffie was preparing to follow she heard a faint stirring behind, and turned just in time to see the dark angel emerge from the small room through which they had passed only seconds before, a puzzled frown on his face as he sniffed suspiciously at the air.

'Fangdrengler!' he snarled. 'Get on out here. I'm sure something putrifyingly good just passed by. I can smell it.'

There was a horrible slurping, gobbling sound, as if someone or something with very bad table manners was trying to cram in as much food as possible all in one go and was choking at the attempt. Then a fat, dribbling demon with the appearance of a dog, which Raffie hadn't noticed before, emerged through the wall behind. 'Here, Master,' he slobbered. 'Right behind you.'

Raffie was so terrified she almost dropped two of the babies. The others, all at the same time, let out a loud squeal of fright. 'Hush!' she said desperately. 'They'll hear.' She knew this was unlikely, given what Aureyel had said about being screened, but, after her encounter with the trainee imp in Wales, she didn't want to run the risk. She had not the slightest desire to take on a fully qualified dark angel along with his demon sidekick. She didn't think she'd stand a chance. She cast one last quick look round, and then catapulted after Josh through the door. But the sight that met her eyes on the other side was hardly more reassuring than the one from which she had just fled.

The laboratory was about six metres square, and crammed from floor to ceiling with shelves and glass-fronted cupboards, all stuffed full with glass bottles and tubes, and strange-looking pieces of equipment whose uses Raffie couldn't even begin to guess at. Down the centre of the room ran a long wooden table that was bolted to the floor with brass screws, its top strewn with dishes, test tubes, microscopes and more of the pieces of equipment that littered the shelves. It was very bright and very clean, and there were two white-coated figures – a man and a woman – standing at the table. They both wore white masks over the lower parts of their faces, and the man was saying, 'So then, do you fancy a drink tonight, or what?'

The woman, transferring something in a pipette from one dish to another, glanced up and said, 'If you like. But I don't want to go to that dive we went to last time. That was horrible.'

It was not any of this, however, that caused Raffie to pull up short, but the presence of what looked at first sight to be a whole regiment of demons and imps. They filled the room, some sitting on shelves, a couple swinging from the fluorescent light overhead, and a whole bevy of them clustered on the tabletop, all avidly watching the woman.

'Raffie,' hissed Josh. 'Over here. We're only just in time. She's just about to fertilize the eggs.'

He seemed almost oblivious to the revolting creatures now pushing and crowding forward towards the dish where the woman worked. Raffie swallowed and said unhappily, 'There's a devil outside. I think he knows we're here.'

'Uh… huh.' Josh was working quickly. He had released the babies from their harnesses and was now lining them up in order on the bench, all the while closely following what the woman was doing. The babies, for their part, were staring wide-eyed up at the demons, and at least three of them looked as if they were about to collapse with terror.

'Josh!' repeated Raffie urgently.

'What?' He looked up.

'I'm sure they know we're here.'

He shook his head impatiently. 'Of course they don't. They know that we have to make a delivery and they'll be expecting something, but they haven't seen us. All hell would have broken loose if they had, so stop worrying. Just get the babies safely in, and then their guardians can take over. Come on!' he added, as Raffie was still standing, staring anxiously round. Whatever Josh said, after seeing the dark angel outside, she felt sure that something was wrong, but she summoned up her courage and joined him over at the bench. 'Don't worry,' he said. 'But we've got to be quick. Put the babies down, and get ready to transfer them the instant fertilization takes place.'

Raffie swallowed hard, but did as Josh directed, and then again glanced anxiously round. A particularly nasty imp, eyes riveted by what the woman was doing and standing so close it was breathing down her neck – if she could have felt it – let out a long hiss. On the bench, the two babies that had been arguing constantly throughout the flight suddenly chose that moment to start a fight. Raffie had no idea why, but they suddenly seemed just to launch themselves at one another, and then tumbled off the bench as both of them slipped under the impact.

'Ee… eurk!' shrieked the imp, as the babies fell out

beyond the confines of the angelic screen. 'There are humans! I can see them!'

A screech of excited fury, like steam exploding through a gasket, burst from all sides. Alerted by the pandemonium, the dark angel from outside shot through the wall, the demon Fangdrengler close on his heels. 'Where?' he spat urgently. 'Where are they?'

But all the demons and imps were now dancing up and down with glee, howling and pointing, and he had no need to search. Raffie had never heard anything like it. They had had a couple of lessons on the nether regions, where the nastier elements of creation commonly lived, up in Cosmological Geography in angel school. The teacher had obligingly opened a viewing window to give them a quick glimpse of what it was actually like, but nothing had prepared her for this. The noise was horrendous, like a thousand dustbin lids all banging together at the same time, along with a malfunctioning loudspeaker system giving off high-pitched screeches and wails. Raffie cringed.

'That's torn it!' said Josh. In one fluid movement he wrenched out his lightning rod, casting aside his invisibility so that the Enemy could see him, and leapt to the babies' defence. Raffie, momentarily stunned, gasped, but the dark angel unfortunately was not so surprised. A look of fiendish glee broke on his face and he drew his sword and sprang forward, while all around him the demons cheered.

Josh was tall and well developed, but he was by no means fully grown. Also, armed as he was only with a lightning rod, compared with the dark angel brandishing the flashing sword in front of him, it looked on all counts to be a rather unequal contest. The fiend at least obviously thought so, because he laughed horribly and bared his rotting teeth. Josh flinched as a stream of foetid breath swept over him, but he gripped his rod more tightly and shouted, 'Back off, fiend! These humans are under protection.'

Unfortunately, the babies he had been carrying also at that moment became visible, so that suddenly the laboratory seemed to be filled with small frenzied bodies running madly this way and that as they tried desperately to avoid the snapping jaws of the now half-crazed demons. Josh glanced at them, distracted, and Raffie knew he was trying desperately to work out which way to jump in order to shield them all at the same time. Seeing his dilemma, the dark angel raised his glittering sword slowly and then crouched down, readying himself for attack. 'Move, angel,' he rasped, his voice like finger nails being dragged across a blackboard. 'You can't match me, and you know it. Stand back! These pathetic little Earthlings are mine! I claim them for the Prince Regent, Metatron!'

'Never!' cried Josh. He sprang forward, sending out a jet of light and striking upwards to parry the blow that the fiend now launched at him.

The movement was enough to release Raffie from her shock, and she too now leapt forwards, grabbing as many of the babies as she could and quickly throwing out a cloud of obscurity to cover them. There was a small 'phut', and all but one disappeared – a baby boy with blond hair and solemn eyes, who looked petrified.

'Hah!' screamed the fiend, looking round in startled surprise. 'There's more than one of you, is there!'

He drew back, sniffing evilly at the air, and Raffie froze as his black eyes raked towards her. But there was no time for fear – Josh was in danger. 'Don't move!' she hissed urgently at the babies, and then she too sprang forward into the air, her body becoming visible, and brandished her rod.

The demons and imps all now went berserk, and Fangdrengler howled with delight. Josh looked at Raffie and smiled – but it wasn't a very confident smile. They moved closer together, stepping forward to meet the inevitable attack. It was not long in coming. The fiend threw himself at them, his sword slicing through the air. Josh only just managed to parry the blow, then he and Raffie sprang either side of their opponent and both lunged together.

'Watch his demon,' panted Josh.

His words came thin and clear into Raffie's mind, like tiny little darts of light, and she knew he was talking at a level the dark forces wouldn't be able to hear. She nodded, too breathless to reply, then ducked as the dark angel again sprang towards her. The baby left alone outside the shield Raffie had thrown over them now scampered round in terror, trying forlornly to hide behind a bank of test tubes. Fangdrengler, eyes flashing fire, followed his every move and then leaped after him, huge jaws snapping hungrily and sending great globules of saliva flying in every direction across the room as he swung his awful head. 'Help!' wailed the baby.

'Oh no!' Josh bounded towards the pair, his rod flashing in a great arc of light that made the air sizzle, and both the dark angel and the imps recoiled. Then an extraordinary thing happened. There was a small blaze of light, which made Fangdrengler start back and howl. And suddenly there was another angel with them in the room. 'Bel!' shouted Josh and Raffie together.

The tall angel blazed towards them, rod furiously swinging this way and that. All around him the demons and imps yowled and leaped back. The first to recover was the black angel. 'Stand your ground, fools!' he bellowed. 'They're only cadets.'

'But how many more of them are there, Master?' whimpered Fangdrengler.

The momentary confusion was all the young angels needed. Raffie, Josh and Bel drew together, forming a wall of defence around the babies; Raffie leaned over and scooped up the last remaining one, dropping him none too gently with his brothers and sisters under the obscurity cloud she had flung over them. 'Jolly glad to see you, Bel,' panted Josh. He looked considerably happier. 'But how in the world did you get here? How did you know?'

Bel laughed grimly. 'Didn't, buddy,' he rejoined. 'Just met some of the others as I was flying back, that was all. They told me what had happened. Said it was funny, so I thought I'd come on down, and see if you needed a hand...'

At that moment, over by the bench, the white-coated woman said to the man, 'You know, Pietro, this batch is being really difficult today. I can't get any of them to gel.'

She put down the hypodermic needle she had been holding. Josh said urgently, 'Get the babies in, Raffie, or it's going to be too late!'

Uncertain what to do, Raffie glanced around. The demons had bunched in again over the row of glass dishes and were slavering and drooling expectantly. Seeing Raffie's hesitation, the dark angel laughed. 'Quite a dilemma, isn't it?' he rasped unpleasantly. 'Stay here and fight me, and they die because they won't get transferred! But fight me, and they'll die anyway, because you don't stand a chance.' The last word ended in a hiss as he again swept up his sword. Then he began to move forward menacingly.

The three angels gulped and instinctively drew closer together. Josh said urgently, 'Go on, Raffie! We've got to get the babies in while there's still a chance. You take them. Bel and I will hold him off.'

Raffie looked at Josh and Bel unhappily, unwilling to desert them, but Bel, a determined glint in his eye, nodded. 'Yeah, you do the business while Josh and I take a turn with this guy here, and then we'll all get out of here!'

She needed no more urging. The dark angel was advancing slowly towards them, Fangdrengler snapping at his heels, so she took a deep breath and disappeared. Immediately she found herself surrounded by clear brightness and light, and the babies all let out a cry of relief. The baby boy she had just rescued whimpered and said, 'What's going to happen? Are we going to be extinguished?'

'No,' said Raffie firmly. 'You're not. You're going to be born, but we've got to be quick.' She scooped them all up in her arms and glided over to stand beside the woman, who was now once again picking up the hypodermic needle and moving it towards the dish while staring down the lens of the microscope. 'One more time,' she remarked wearily, 'and if I can't get them to go in now, we'll call it a day. It must be a bad batch.'

Raffie gathered the babies together and said quietly, 'OK now, get ready...' Elsewhere in the room there was a loud yell and what sounded like the clash of steel, and then a cascade of sparks fountained into the air. Raffie ignored them. Whatever else might be happening, what was going on in front of her now was equally important. If she missed this moment, as the dark angel had pointed out, it would be too late, but if she could get the babies in they would all have a chance. Holding her breath, she watched as the woman very carefully inserted the tip of the needle into a cell, and then slowly pushed... 'OK!' said Raffie. She picked up the baby boy who was still staring at her apprehensively and, with equal care, slid him very, very carefully towards the dish.

'I don't believe it!' gasped the woman. 'Did you see that? It just sort of slid in, easy as pie... all by itself! And after all the trouble we've had!'

Beside her the man laughed. 'Told you there was nothing to worry about. Get the others done quick, and then we can go and have that drink.'

Within ten minutes, all sixteen babies were safely transferred into what were now tiny embryos. 'Bye!' called out Holly, who was the last to go in. 'Will I see you again?'

'Bye,' called back Raffie. 'Maybe... maybe not... but I'll be around.'

She watched as the baby girl nestled into her new form and waved, and then turned back to see what was going on in the room behind. The two white-coated workers were now packing everything away but, more importantly for Raffie, the demons and imps, who only moments before had been clustered drooling over the bench, had now drawn back and were beginning to disperse.

In the centre of the room, however, a terrible and rather one-sided battle was raging as Josh and Bel fought desperately to try to keep the dark angel away. In fact, they'd have been slaughtered immediately if it hadn't been for the presence of the seething mass of imps, who were so excited at what was going on that they kept getting under the Enemy angel's feet and tripping him up. Raffie felt a shiver of horror, but she was no coward, so she took a fresh grip on her lightning rod, preparing to join her friends in what she felt would be certain annihilation. At that moment, however, a rather extraordinary thing happened. A long clear blast from a trumpet rang out through the air and the dark angel jerked upright, transfixed.

Raffie blinked, uncertain what it meant, but Bel sprang back jubilantly and yelled, 'Watchers! At last!'

The dark angel realized that too. He spun away, sheathing his sword, and summoning Fangdrengler with an angry flick of his head. He spat, 'We'll meet again, angelings. Make no mistake. This is not finished yet. You do not cross Azariel and survive! I shall still have those humans!' And then, with a loud bang, he disappeared.

There was another loud, pealing blast, followed by a wind like a mini tornado, and into the room erupted two magnificent and brilliant angels, swords raised. 'Lucis!' exclaimed Raffie, almost crying with relief as she recognized her mentor. 'You're here.'

Seeing Lucis, Josh and Bel sank weakly to their knees, holding each other up in relief. 'Thank heavens!' gasped Josh. 'I thought we'd had it!' They collapsed forward into each other's arms, brushing their wings – which is what angels do when they want to congratulate each other. Raffie, feeling a relief she wouldn't have imagined possible, ran across and threw herself onto them. 'You're all right!' she cried ecstatically. 'Thank goodness!'

All three clutched each other. As soon as he was sufficiently recovered, Bel said to Raffie, 'You did it, then?'

Raffie nodded joyfully, but from the corner of her eye noticed that Lucis was now walking grimly round the laboratory, noting closely where all the demons and imps had last been. When he came to the place where the dark angel had disappeared, he paused, glanced across at them and said, 'This one was one of the dark lords – one of the inner Council by the smell of it.' He whistled softly and said, 'Who was it? Did you get a name?'

The three of them pulled apart reluctantly and stood up, grinning at each other. After all the excitement, they could hardly believe that they were all still in one piece. 'Yes, he did say his name,' Josh said. 'It was something like Azariel, I think, or –'

'Azariel!'

Both the Watchers spun round, clearly startled, and a look shot between the two of them. 'Azariel!' breathed the other, staring intently at Lucis, a strange expression on his face. 'I wouldn't have thought it possible. Why in heaven's name should he be here?'

'I don't know.' Lucis shook his head. A worried frown settled on his face. He looked across at the three probationers and said curtly, 'Did you deliver all the humans safely?'

Disconcerted, Raffie didn't immediately answer but then, a little uncertainly, said, 'Yes, they're all over there… in those tubes.'

'Really?' The two Watchers walked over to the bench. Lucis stared down at them and said thoughtfully, 'One of these must be very important for the Enemy to have singled him or her out for so much attention, so soon. But the question is… which one, and why?'

The other angel said, 'I can't tell. They all look the same to me. I think we ought to go and check with Records.' He glanced at Lucis, who nodded in agreement then said, 'But I think we ought to post a guard down here too. If one of these humans is that important, the Enemy isn't going to give up that easily, is he?'

7
A Welcome Break?

'I think you ought to take a holiday, Raffie,' said Lucis. 'In fact, I think all three of you could do with a holiday after that fiasco. You were very, very lucky to have survived. We can't be everywhere all at the same time, you know. Even Watchers.' He shook his head in despair and said for what seemed the hundredth time, 'To survive a contest with Azariel… It's beyond belief!'

They were back up in one of the rooms of BABE, awaiting the arrival of Madame Germinel, who had apparently almost exploded when informed of all that had happened. Bel shifted his feet uncomfortably and said, 'But it isn't like we chose to have a contest with him.'

This was apparently the wrong thing to say, because Lucis glared at him and said, 'I'd keep quiet about that if I were you, Libertybel. As I understand it, your assignment was to Asia, and you shouldn't have been anywhere near Rome.'

Josh and Raffie looked at each other, and Raffie burst out indignantly, 'But Lucis, if he hadn't come, we'd have been annihilated! That dark angel saw us and…'

'And that's another thing,' interrupted Lucis coldly. 'Exactly why had you and Joshuel thrown off your screening? You know perfectly well that in the normal course of events you would have remained completely invisible to those creatures through the whole operation.

We go to a lot of trouble up at headquarters to maintain constant angelic screening from all Enemy surveillance, and the only way that they could possibly have spotted you would be if you had voluntarily thrown off your cover.'

His chin, which was rather large and determined, jutted out accusingly, and Raffie wilted. 'It was the babies,' she said in a small voice. 'Two of them were fighting… and…'

'And they fell out of the cover,' carried on Josh. 'The demons saw them and went for them, and so I materialized to protect them…'

'And then Azariel went for Joshuel,' ended Raffie, 'so I went to help him.'

Lucis looked as if he could hardly believe his ears but, perhaps thankfully, at that moment Madame Germinel came in. She looked flustered, her halo askew and wing feathers standing on end, and she threw up her hands as her eyes fell on Raffie, Josh and Bel and exclaimed, 'Ah, *quelle désastre*! What a terrible thing to 'appen! That terrible angel… Are you all right?'

She threw her arms round them, clutching them to her ample bosom. Josh blushed as he tried to extricate himself and said, 'We're fine, thank you, ma'am.'

Madame Germinel ignored him. 'And the babies?' she went on, kissing each one of the three angels in turn. 'I am told that they are all safe too. Ah, what a miracle! You have done well, all of you!'

Lucis cleared his throat loudly at this point, clearly annoyed at the bestowal of so much praise when he had just been doing his best to tell them off. Madame

Germinel spun round, for the first time becoming aware of the tall Watcher, standing at the side. 'Ah, Lucis!' she exclaimed, rushing across and embracing him too, planting a resounding kiss on either cheek. 'She has done well, your little charge. You must be proud!'

Lucis looked anything but proud. In fact Raffie thought he looked as if he was about to explode, but he controlled himself and growled, 'Well, at least they're all in one piece.'

'One piece! Ah, *alors*!' exclaimed Madame Germinel, totally unabashed. 'Much more than that, I think. They have got the babies in safe. Their guardians are all with them now. Four will be born. That is good.'

Raffie stared at her. Like the others, she felt rather overcome by the explosive energy of the buxom little archangel, and wondered for a moment if she had heard right. 'Four?' she asked tentatively. 'But we took down sixteen…'

Madame Germinel shrugged. 'Yes, I know. But it is the… 'ow you say, the IVF treatment. Only the four have been implanted. The rest have been frozen. It is good. They will stay there now until needed, I think, but there is no danger. I will get them back as soon as possible and they will either stay here up in heaven, where they will be 'appy, or they will be reassigned.'

Raffie could hardly believe her ears. IVF or not, only four implanted! She thought back to how lively all the babies had been, and wondered which ones. Would Holly have been one of them? she wondered. Or would she now be inert in some giant deep freeze, waiting reselection? And what about the human that the Enemy apparently thought so important – where was he or she? This thought was apparently also on Lucis' mind, because he raised a brow and enquired, 'And the…?'

'Yes, yes!' Madame Germinel said quickly, holding up a hand to stop him from saying any more. 'All is well. 'Ave I not said? Our problem now is to decide what to do with our young angels here.' She turned back to the three juniors standing in front of her and said firmly, 'You must have rest. You have done very well, all of you… I am especially pleased, Libertybel, that you went to the aid of your friends. But now you must all have a break and get away from this excitement for a while.'

She beamed, as if this settled everything, and said energetically, 'You will have an 'oliday. When you come back, we will think what to do with you next.'

'I'm not sure I really want a holiday,' said Raffie to Lucis later. 'I don't seem to have been assigned very long. I think I'd rather just carry on and try to get more of a feel of things.'

Lucis shook his head, but Raffie was relieved to see that he no longer seemed annoyed. 'No, it's better this way,' he replied. 'You've been involved in rather too much excitement, all of you. It was bad enough when you took on that imp down in Wales, but to have got caught up in a battle with Azariel… First level angels, as I've explained to you before, are expressly forbidden to become active participants in Enemy engagements. You're not trained. Of course,' he added grudgingly, 'It's true that you did do rather well – in the circumstances. But HQ feels now that you definitely ought to take a rest. I know you don't feel it, but this kind of thing can actually be a real strain, especially when there's any kind of engagement with one of the dark lords, and they're very concerned up top that none of you suffer from post traumatic angelic stress.'

Raffie frowned. 'Who is Azariel exactly?' she asked. 'And why does everyone seem so astonished that he was down there?'

Lucis shook his head, as if refusing to answer, but then he seemed to think better of it, and he said slowly, 'Azariel was a very high-ranking Watcher who first staged a mutiny with Metatron, the Regent, back before the Great Rebellion. He was one of the leaders, in fact, and it's rumoured he first came up with the plan of trying to corrupt humans – which Metatron's been using so brilliantly ever since. Now he heads up the Enemy Special Forces, who engage in undercover and terrorist operations.' He looked at her closely and said firmly, 'And more than that, you really do not want to know. In fact the best thing now would be for you just to forget all of this and take that break we've been talking about. Then, when you come back, you can concentrate on your training.'

But where to go? That was the problem. Faced with so much choice, Raffie found it almost impossible to decide. Bel announced that he was going to go off to the West Coast of the United States and that, after that, he thought he'd take in a couple of the National Parks, Yosemite maybe, or Yellowstone. He liked North America, he explained. Josh said that on the whole he was a bit tired of Earth, after so much excitement, so he thought he'd go and have a quick gander around the stars. There was an especially fascinating area around the Andromeda system, he added enthusiastically, that he'd been meaning to visit for aeons. But Raffie had absolutely no idea where to go. She felt she didn't know enough of what there was anywhere to be able to choose. She didn't even know the names of many places yet.

She decided in the end to fly back over Europe and see if anything caught her eye, so as the sun was lifting over the horizon she flew with Josh and Bel as far as the North Pole, and then they all went their separate ways. 'See you in a couple of Earth weeks,' shouted Josh gaily, a long vapour trail of light fanning out behind him as he sped away. 'Don't do anything I wouldn't do...'

Raffie waved, and then headed back towards Italy. But it wasn't long before her attention was caught by a particularly attractive frilly bit of coastline that seemed to weave inwards to form a mesh of what looked to be lakes, and so she flew down lower to investigate. She found that the ground below formed a kind of high plateau, covered with thick floes of ice and freshly fallen snow. It looked very cold, and there seemed to be no one there. Then here and there she noticed some rather forlorn-looking reindeer nibbling dejectedly at the snow. Poor things, she thought, staring at them and wondering if there was anything she could do to help. But apart from leading them to a patch of more fertile ground that she had spotted where the grass was just beginning to poke through, there didn't seem anything, and so after a while she flew on.

She passed over water, land, more water, and then a patchwork of green and brown fields, interspersed with woods and clusters of towns. In a few places she saw signs of Enemy activity, and she avoided these, mindful of

Lucis's advice. By late in the Earth day she was beginning to grow tired and she started to look around, anxious for somewhere to stop. At last she spotted a long rolling hill, its top crowned with a fringe of trees, almost like a monk's shaved head, and with a stream of bright water gushing merrily down the side towards the thickly wooded valley far below. What actually drew her attention, however, were several long lines of people trailing laboriously up the hill towards the bald area at the top. There was already a throng there and, when she listened hard, Raffie could hear laughter and faint snatches of song. Her curiosity piqued, she flew down and perched on a small rocky outcrop that overlooked the crowd, giving her a clear view of the valley rolling away far below.

It was very pleasant out on the sun-baked hill. The late afternoon rays of the sun had warmed the rock and a gentle breeze that seemed alive with butterflies and small gnats wafted across the slope, humming with vibrant life. It reminded Raffie of the heavens and all that she had left, and she stretched luxuriously, wondering what was going on. The people meanwhile streamed in, chattering excitedly, then gathering together and flopping down in small groups. Their mood seemed expectant, and Raffie stared around, wondering what they were waiting for.

This, she realized, was how she had always imagined Earth would be. Peaceful and quiet, the sun streaming down, no hint of anything untoward. In this she was not quite right, however, because she soon noticed that there were little groups of imps, invisible, of course, in the natural world, but who had come up with various people and were now all clustering at the side, biting and spitting at each other and generally shouting abuse. Even they, however, didn't seem very interested in doing anything too energetic, and after a while Raffie relaxed and sat back, watching to see what would happen next.

She had not long to wait. A ripple of excitement ran round the crowd, and then a group of about twenty men and women appeared over the side of the hill. In their middle walked a tall man, who seemed to be the leader, although he was dressed just like all the rest of them in rough looking trousers and a dark jacket, with a cap on his head. They came right to the centre, just below where Raffie was perched, and then the tall man stood forward and lifted up his arms. 'Friends!' he called out, and his voice seemed to carry the entire length of the hill. 'Friends! Welcome to the first meeting of our revolutionary congress…'

Over by the head of the stream, where it gushed merrily out of the Earth, the imps looked up and scowled, but then, clearly not overly interested in the scene being played out below, they began to settle down. The man launched into a passionate speech. To Raffie's surprise the reaction of the crowd now seemed rather mixed. Some of the listeners, it was true, seemed to be drinking in every word excitedly, but others seemed hostile, and there were a few boos and jeers. Puzzled, Raffie leaned forward, craning to hear, and she heard the man shout, 'We have fought for our freedom, but now we must fight to turn out the foreign aggressors and once again re-establish true belief. We must cleanse the infidel from our midst!'

Now thoroughly interested, Raffie leaned further forward, chin on hand, but the happy mood of the crowd seemed to be changing, and she could almost feel the deep rumbles of anger that were growing on all sides. The man too seemed to notice this, because he became even more passionate, hotly denouncing the evils of foreign influence which had led to the corruption of their culture. Listening intently, Raffie decided that he must be some sort of local warlord. But it was equally clear that not everybody liked him, because from all sides now there rose a growing murmur of angry discontent. 'Go home, Nikolai!' shouted a man's voice. 'We're tired of all this talk of war. We want peace!'

'You are weak!' shouted back the man furiously. 'Unless we defend our traditional values, there can't ever be any peace.'

It was all most perplexing, and Raffie found herself craning further and further forward, trying to follow what was going on. Quite when the transformation happened she wasn't sure, but suddenly she became aware that a shocked silence had fallen on the crowd, and that they were all gazing up towards her with mingled expressions of wonder and dread. Surprised, she rose to her feet and stared around, shaking out her wings and peering round to try to see what it was that had caught the crowd's attention. And then, to her horror, she realized exactly what it was. Her! She had no idea when it had happened but, sometime while the people were arguing, she must have become so engrossed in what was going on that, straining towards them, she had somehow let herself slip into visibility, becoming obvious both to the Enemy and to the crowds on the hill.

Alerted by the sudden silence, over in the long grass a

couple of minor imps who had been tormenting an ant looked up lazily, and then jerked to attention. 'Blimey!' exclaimed one, 'it's an angel.'

'Cor, you're right!' replied the other, almost hopping up and down with excitement. 'You're not wrong... There must be something really big going down for the Enemy to materialize like that.' Then it rubbed its moon-like, vicious little eyes, as if still not quite believing them, and demanded, 'What d'ya think we ought to do then?'

The pair, maddened at finding themselves in such close proximity to an angelic being from the other side, started arguing, and a small ring of their fellow imps, attracted by the noise, quickly gathered round them. All now joined in, and within moments a full-scale row erupted. Some expressed the opinion that they ought to go and tell the boss so that Special Forces could come and deal with it. 'After all,' screeched one particularly verminous looking creature, 'that's what they say they're trained for, great useless lumps of lard! Let them deal with it!' But others took the view that this was a rather wimpish approach. And then matters disintegrated into chaos when another imp wandered up and, rather impetuously, expressed the view that the first speaker was a big girl's blouse, at which point the debate became a fight. By the time some sort of order was restored, the mood of the group was definitely inclining towards an immediate full-frontal assault.

Raffie, meanwhile, simply continued to stand there, frozen with horror as the full implications of what she had done began to sink in. How was she going to explain this to Lucis? He would be furious. Unauthorized fighting with demons and dark angels was bad enough, but an unlicensed visitation? She'd be lucky to keep her wings after this!

While she was trying to work out what to do, however, a strange kind of transformation was taking place among the crowd. A low 'Aaah!' of awe went up, gradually rising to a crescendo. Then all over the hillside men and women began to fall to their knees, some calling out that it was judgment and moaning crazily; others loudly begging protection from God, the ruling political party or anything that might be able to promise them deliverance. Raffie felt even more surprised. They were, she realized, absolutely terrified, but why? Then the man who had spoken at such length, and who had fallen over when he first saw her, staggered back to his feet and ran forward into the crowd, arms once again raised, and shouted, 'Don't worry! It's not real! It must be a capitalist plot. It'll all be done by lights!'

Raffie felt rather offended. Nobody had ever levelled this kind of insult at her before. But the next minute an unidentifiable voice shouted back, 'Idiot! You don't know what you're talking about, Nikolai. It's a visitation from God!'

Over by the stream, the imps, further maddened by the demonstration of reverence that Raffie's appearance now threatened to provoke, came to an abrupt and unanimous decision to attack. The more vociferous among them screeched and yowled horrifically, and they launched themselves en masse, jaws snapping and slavering, talons thrashing at the ground, tumbling and falling over each other in a race to be the first to grab the angel and tear her to pieces.

The first Raffie knew of it was a black tide of spitting, snarling furies, all headed in her direction. Appalled, she rose a metre in the air, raised a hand to ward off the attack… and then dematerialized.

All around, the crowd went wild. They took Raffie's abrupt disappearance as absolute confirmation of what the unknown voice had just said, and a large turnip whistled through the air, catching the enraged revolutionary neatly on the ear. 'You're mad!' shouted back the target, even more furious at this. 'You're deceived! It's just an optical delusion, I tell you!'

But the crowd didn't care. Without exception, they now decided that the celestial vision which had been hovering above them, hand raised in apparent blessing, was a sign from God – even though many of them up to that point had always said that they didn't believe in God. 'Go home!' they shouted. 'Stuff your revolution, Nikolai. We don't want to fight!'

Now, again invisible to the crowd but still in main view of the demons, Raffie catapulted up into the air, gasping for breath and almost choking with panic. There was going to be trouble over this, she knew. Behind her, imps (also of course invisible to the men and women on the hillside) howled angrily as their talons closed on the empty space that only moments before had been full of angel. Unable themselves to fly, they fought and clawed at each other, straining upwards to try to reach her before she could get away. Raffie was terrified. She cast one more frightened glance back and then beat urgently upwards with her wings, struggling to rise. But she was still stunned and found she could manage no more than a feeble flutter, which only raised her another metre or so. Seeing her difficulty, and determined she should not get away, some of the imps screamed with delight and began to clamber up on top of each other, forming a kind of swaying, rickety ladder that lurched drunkenly towards her feet.

'Aah!' moaned Raffie, feeling claws brush the hem of her robes.

'Ooh!' moaned the crowd in unconscious imitation.

'Stop this!' yelled Nikolai, almost dancing up and down with rage.

And then an extraordinary thing happened. Just as a talon tore through the hem of Raffie's robe and she was beginning to despair, a giant hand suddenly reached down and grabbed hold of her, lifting her high into the air. Then there was a brilliant flash of light, like the explosion of a star, and the maddened imps who had been clustered below suddenly scattered like shards of blasted glass.

Relief flooding through her, though confused at what was happening, Raffie gulped great lungfuls of air and struggled to steady herself. But just as she managed to gather herself into some sort of order, a shadow loomed over her and a voice boomed, 'Angel! What are you doing here?'

For a moment, this was almost more frightening than first sight of the imps rushing towards her. Raffie winced, but then plucked up her courage and, very timidly, looked round. The sight that met her eyes made her gasp. Behind her was a very large and very annoyed-looking Cherub, with two only slightly smaller looking Watchers standing either side, all of them in full battle dress, their bodies surrounded by a flaming aureole of light. As if this were not bad enough, however, great golden flashes seemed also to burst and crackle intermittently from the edges of the Cherub's wings, so that he looked as if he was about to explode. None of them, Raffie realized with a sinking heart, looked at all pleased. 'Er... um... h... hello,' she faltered, feeling something was expected of her.

But whatever that was, this clearly wasn't it. The expression on the face of the Cherub hardened, and he repeated, 'What are you doing here, angel? This is a restricted sector, classified as highly dangerous. Access is forbidden to all angels below the rank of Watcher, unless entering with special authority. Didn't you see the signs? How did you get here?'

Raffie gazed at him stupidly, her head beginning to swim. Restricted sector? Access forbidden unless with special authority? She hadn't the slightest idea what he was talking about. It was true she had felt puzzled when she had seen no other angels flying around, but after a while she had decided that that was maybe the way it was down on Earth. Rather empty. And then she had felt pleased, glad of the chance to be alone at last and have opportunity to try to make sense of all that had happened up at BABE. But the furious Cherub in front of her seemed to be suggesting something rather different, and Raffie blinked at him, appalled. 'Authority?' she repeated. 'What authority? I didn't know I needed authority... I'm just taking a holiday.'

'A holiday!' The word seemed jerked from the Cherub with all the force of a popped cork. He articulated it with bafflement, as if the syllables were somehow alien, knitted together into a word that he had never come across before.

Then a glazed look settled across his features, and he said with more restraint, 'Why in the name of all that's sacred should you be taking a holiday? You're a junior, aren't you?'

If Raffie had felt bad before, she felt now as if she had been suddenly plunged into an icy lake of skin-stripping sulphur (angels don't like sulphur. Everything on Earth has its counterpart in the heavens, and for them sulphur is like acid. It burns). But to Raffie, the Cherub pronounced the word 'junior' as if she belonged to some kind of subspecies for which the idea of a holiday was not only irrelevant but absurd. She cringed and glanced quickly away, wondering if there was any way she could avoid recounting all that had happened. In the same instant, her eyes fell on a curious little tableau now being enacted on the ground far below. The man called Nikolai seemed to be running backwards and forwards in increasing agitation, gesticulating wildly and trying to get the crowd's attention. The people, however, seemed to be equally as determined to ignore him, and all over the hillside men and women were on their knees, some with expressions of rapture on their faces, a few in tears.

Interesting though all this appeared to Raffie, however, the Cherub seemed unimpressed. He followed her eyes down and gave a quick 'Tck!' of impatience. When she looked back, she found him glaring at her stonily. 'I'm waiting, angel,' he said.

Raffie swallowed, uttered a quick but silent prayer – which, however, judging by the lack of result, didn't seem to have been heard – then began to recount all that had happened since she had first been assigned. But putting the tale into words only made it seem even more awful. The Cherub was right, Raffie realized: junior angels should not need a holiday – but then again, most junior angels didn't find themselves in combat with demons and imps, and all as a result of their own stupidity. Feeling more and more miserable, she ploughed on. When she got to the part about Azariel, she thought she heard the Cherub give a quick intake of breath and noticed the Watchers exchange a look. It was a peculiar kind of look, veiled and apprehensive at the same time, but with something else mixed in that she couldn't identify. Just then, however, her puzzlement was entirely forgotten, because the Watcher on the left suddenly sprang forward, eyes straining into the distance, and hissed urgently, 'Raguel! They're coming. I can feel them!'

All three of them spun round and stared in the direction the Watcher was now pointing, and Raffie felt the two powerful angels beside her tense. Frightened, she too peered upwards, straining to see what it was that had caught their attention. But try as she might, she could make out nothing. The sky looked spectacular, with the sun beginning to sink below the horizon in a ball of flaming fire, and the deep blue of early evening shading into purple-fingered night. And then she saw it, a tiny pinprick of darkness – so black, it was like an absence of life – moving swiftly towards them as it crossed the line of the dying sun.

It moved rapidly, growing in size, and after a moment the Cherub said quietly, 'Unless I'm very much mistaken, that's the one we've just been talking about. Come to see how his protegée is getting on, I expect.'

For one horrible moment Raffie thought that he was referring to her and was about to protest, but then she saw him glance briefly towards the Watchers and realized that none of them were bothered about her any more, so she shut her mouth quickly.

Raguel said tersely, 'OK, lads, cloaking screens on. Now.' He nodded towards Raffie. 'You too... do you know how to use one?'

'No.' Raffie shook her head dumbly. For a moment she thought she must have tumbled into some kind of horrible dream, and had to suppress an insane desire to laugh. This couldn't be happening! The look on Raguel's face, however, told her that it was, and she muttered, 'First level angels don't receive combat training, sir.'

That at least was completely unarguable. Raffie had heard of the cloaking devices routinely used by the Watchers and Cherubs, of course, but she had never actually come across them before, and certainly didn't understand how they worked. She knew that they were used to screen the operational presence of the Host (which was the name given to the angelic Special Forces) from Enemy surveillance, and that they acted in much the same way as the screens she, Josh and Libertybel had been assigned up at BABE. Unlike those screens, however, she knew that the ones used by the elite forces were far more powerful and could be controlled almost like a weapon. And then Raffie suddenly realized why she hadn't known they were there before. They must have been cloaked when she arrived, and all the time she was sitting on the rock. They had been screened from her too!

She watched stupefied as the Watchers obediently

unfurled long cloaks from the bags slung across their fronts and cast them in one quick movement over their shoulders, instantly disappearing from view. Raguel nodded and said tersely, 'All right. Get behind me and make sure you stay close. Whatever you do, keep out of sight.' Then he seemed to take pity on her, because he added, 'Don't worry, we're not here to engage the Enemy. We've just been ordered to observe.'

8
The Dark Forces

Raffie slipped gratefully under the cloak the huge Cherub now threw about his shoulders. It was an extraordinary experience, like stepping into a pool of fluid, luminous light. One moment she was out in the open, the next the air around her seemed to shimmer and there was a cold breath of wind, and she found herself suddenly in a kind of half world that was full of brightness. Full of a funny kind of noise, too. This was unexpected and, crouched down where Raguel indicated, Raffie tilted her head, trying to locate where it was coming from. But try as she might, she couldn't, because it seemed to be everywhere: a low, strange kind of harmonious hum. After a moment she realized that it was the angels talking to one another.

'It's the big guy, sure enough,' she made out, and was surprised to recognize a voice not dissimilar to Libertybel's. And then another voice replied, 'Yes, several dozen support troops with him too, by the looks of it.'

'Quiet!' said Raguel brusquely. 'All non verbal communications stop now. Maintain airwave silence.'

Safe under the shadow of the Cherub's wings, Raffie looked around curiously. She could see everything outside the cloaking device perfectly but, more surprisingly, she found she could also see the Watchers. Then she blinked with astonishment – there were not just two with Raguel, but six, huge and grim, and all standing alert as they leaned lightly on their great swords, watching impassively the approach of the black cloud. Raffie had never been so close to what she now realized was an elite unit of the Host, and she felt awestruck. Just wait till she told Josh and Bel about this! Both of them, she knew, harboured ambitions to become Watchers, and they'd be wild with envy when she told them.

The cloud rolled relentlessly towards them, and now Raffie could make out the dark angels banded together in ranks, all of them with attendant demons snapping at their heels. There seemed to be dozens of them. At their head she saw Azariel. She recognized him instantly, his huge blue-black, onyx-tipped wings and the glittering circlet that bound his raven hair making him stand out. Even from a distance away she shivered and, as if reading her thoughts, Raguel glanced round briefly and said softly, 'Don't worry, angel. I know he looks pretty fearsome, but he's not going to hurt you.'

Surprised, she looked up at him gratefully and he gave a quick half-smile before turning back to watch the approach of the oncoming foe.

Raffie felt stunned by it all. There were so many questions tumbling around her mind. Why was the Enemy so clearly visible? Didn't they have cloaking devices too? And why were there so many demons with them? But now was clearly not the right time to ask and, with a growing feeling of dread, she reached out and grasped a handful of Raguel's robe for reassurance. But if the mighty Cherub felt it, he gave no sign, and so Raffie just crouched down behind, wishing that Azariel and all his dark forces would change their minds and go away.

But they didn't, and the noise as they drew near was terrible. Whereas the Watchers had seemed to hum to one another gently, in what had sounded at first to Raffie like music, the Enemy Special Forces seemed to snap and snarl, and there were constant barked commands and growls. They swept up onto the crown of the bald hill like a plague of black locusts. The imps who were already there, having arrived earlier with their human hosts, began to cheer and hop around excitedly, but Azariel's ebony face darkened even more when he took in the crowds, most of whom were still wailing and crying, hands outstretched in supplication towards the spot where Raffie had so recently appeared.

'What's going on?' he demanded of the imps, now running hither and thither over the ground in dribbling anticipation. And Raffie heard again those terrible tones, like nails being dragged across a blackboard, that she remembered so well from the laboratory back in Rome, and that she had hoped never to hear ever again.

At Azariel's feet Fangdrengler ran round in frenzied circles, snuffling excitedly at the ground. The dark angel looked down at him and barked, 'What is it, Fang? What do you smell?'

Arriving at the rock on which Raffie had perched, the demon hound raised his slavering head and growled, 'Angel, master! I smell angel!'

This was clearly not what Azariel had expected, because he started and walked forward, staring intently at the rock. 'What... here?' he asked. 'There's been an angel here? Are you sure?'

His tone expressed disbelief, but Fangdrengler nodded

his great head vehemently, globules of saliva flying in all directions from his gaping jaws, and repeated, 'Yes, Master. It's the same smell I smelled back in Rome.'

'What!' Azariel's eyes narrowed, and the thin slits of his pupils scanned the ground rapidly. The imps, who had by now registered that something was badly wrong, and who clearly thought that in this particular instance discretion would definitely be the better part of valour, began to try to melt away. They slid and crawled under nearby rocks and tussocks of grass. The dark angel's voice suddenly barked out, 'Stay where you are!'

It was as if a film had been put on pause. The imps all jerked upright and froze, and Azariel spun round and glared at them. Then, very slowly, he began to pace across the ground, chin on hand.

Out on the hillside, some of the men and women who had been making rather feeble attempts to address the fabulous being who had so recently appeared now began to sing, a not very tuneful rendition of an old hymn. Azariel scowled. He walked round slowly, pausing every so often to examine a particular individual more closely – clearly revolted by all he saw. Then at last he came to Nikolai, and a softer expression settled on his face. The revolutionary leader was still shouting and beating uselessly at the air with his fists, hurling insults at the crowd and at what he branded their sheep-like mentality. When Azariel got to him, the dark angel stopped approvingly and said softly, almost like a purr, 'And you, my pet... my own... what do you say has happened here? Was there truly an angel?'

To Raffie's astonishment, it was almost as if the man on

the ground heard, because he raised his eyes, groaning, and cried out in tones of despair, 'An angel! Yes… An angel! How can they be so naïve?'

The effect on Azariel was instantaneous. He recoiled as if he had been stung, giving a great gasp of rasping breath, and Raffie heard Raguel give an exclamation of annoyance. Agitated herself, she tried to stand, but the Cherub reached behind to restrain her, signalling to her to be still. Azariel spun back round and shouted at the imps, 'Is this really so? *Was* there an angel here?'

For answer, the imps all began to nod and jabber excitedly. The noise was horrendous, and for a moment it felt as if bedlam had broken out. Azariel was furious. 'Silence!' he shouted. 'I can't hear a thing in all this racket!' His eyes swept round angrily, and finally came to rest on a runtish little imp that was clinging to the ground and that had so far said nothing but had an intelligent face. 'You,' he commanded, 'Tell me what has gone on here. Why do our plans seem to have gone so badly astray?'

The imp, finding itself the unwelcome centre of attention, writhed and tried ineffectually to worm its way into the ground. Even more annoyed, Azariel aimed a stinging blast of black light straight at its head, and it pulled sharply back, rubbing at its singed neck with an air of affront. 'All right, all right,' it protested. 'Go easy. No need for that…' Azariel raised his arm again and the imp said hastily, 'Yes, Your Worship, as it happens, there was an angel here.' And then it went on in an oily tone, 'But an insignificant sort of an angel, Your Anti-Holiness, sir… very small and mean looking… with a very sickly kind of light. Not at all like YOUR WORSHIP here!'

Clearly enraged at such obvious toadying towards his master, Fangdrengler chose that moment to snap hungrily at the imp, who gave a loud shriek, diving for cover behind Nikolai's legs. 'Leave him, Fang!' shouted Azariel. 'I want to hear what he's got to say!' He aimed another jet of black light at the demon dog by way of reinforcement, and it withdrew, howling. Azariel said broodingly, 'An angel... A small angel... with the same smell that we came across in Rome... Is that possible?'

He turned towards the first rank of dark angels now hovering behind and barked, 'What do you all think? Do we have intelligence of any Enemy activity in this area?'

The angels, who looked to Raffie like rather dark, but still undeniably beautiful, shadows of the Watchers, shuffled uneasily. At last, one of them plucked up courage to say, 'No reports, sir, but you know as well as we do that that doesn't mean they're not around. You know we can't penetrate their defence systems.'

Raffie almost expected another blast of fury to greet this reply, but instead she was astonished to see Azariel merely scowl, and then mutter, 'The Host, yes it's true. We can't track them... but, if Fang is right, those angels in Rome weren't combat level. They were trainees, and we should have picked them up immediately... so what's going on?' He seemed to sink into a kind of reverie, and Raffie heard him muttering, 'Obviously the Tyrant must have got wind that we're planning an offensive. Why else would he order a manifestation here? But to use one of the angels from Rome? It doesn't make sense... What can the connection be?' His head jerked up suddenly and he snapped, 'Are you sure you've got it right, Fang? Are you certain it's the same scent?'

The demon nodded sulkily, and moved from behind the rock where he had taken refuge. He was clearly still smarting from the blow Azariel had aimed at him, but he roused himself sufficiently to hiss, ' 'Course I'm sure, Master. It was a particularly vile stink of innocent holiness. Turned my stomach, it did! I'm not sure, but I think it was the little one.'

Though safely hidden behind Raguel, Raffie felt her wings turn to jelly. But that was nothing to the way she felt next, because Azariel suddenly wheeled round, his piercing, feline eyes raking the air as if trying to find her then fixing directly on a spot just above her head. For one horrible moment Raffie thought that, whatever the protection afforded by Raguel's cloak, the dark angel could see her; at her side, she felt Raguel tense and grip his sword.

But just as suddenly, Azariel looked away and muttered, 'There are things I don't understand here, Fang. If you're right, then maybe the Enemy is planning a counter-attack. After all, he likes the *feeble*.' Azariel spat the word with loathing. 'He's used them time and again in the past, and always when he's got something really vile planned. So maybe what we're seeing here is the start of a counter-surveillance undercover op... Maybe that pathetic runt of an angel in Rome wasn't quite what she seemed after all!'

Raffie couldn't help it. She gave a whimper of terror, and Raguel instantly spun round and clamped a hand over her mouth. 'Ssh!' he hissed urgently into her ear. 'Although they can't see us, some sound bleeds through. Do you want him to hear?'

She shook her head, now almost speechless with panic,

and the Cherub nodded to her to watch, a grim smile curling his lips. Obediently Raffie looked down and saw Azariel now issuing rapid commands to his troops. But, from the blank expressions on their faces, it looked like none of them had a clue what he was talking about. Unable to help herself, Raffie stared at them, fascinated. If she had never previously been so close to a unit of Watchers, she had certainly never encountered a group of Enemy elite troops before. Indeed, she'd never even seen them from a distance, and tried dimly to recall what she'd heard about them.

She wasn't entirely sure, but she thought that the Enemy counterpart to Watchers were called Tempters – but they'd had so little information on this group up in angel school that she wasn't sure if she'd got that right or not. She did know, however, that they were angels who had rebelled a long time ago, and that they served Metatron, the dark Cherub who was their leader, and who'd been appointed Regent to Earth by the High King himself. As Gabriel had told her when he'd approved her posting, after the Regent had revolted and declared independence, claiming the planet for himself, all the other disaffected angels and spirits from the whole of creation had gathered around him, and now they used Earth as their headquarters – though the evil they did spread far beyond.

Beyond that Raffie hadn't the slightest idea what they did, and had certainly never realized that in appearance they might be different. And yet different they most certainly were. They were tall and powerful – just like the Watchers. But whereas Watchers seemed to radiate a kind of intense white power, there was about these angels a concentrated, shining darkness that made her skin crawl with dread. There was something decadent and corrupt about them, and the forms of some looked as if they were beginning to decay. But some were also strangely beautiful, with dark, chiselled features and eyes that seemed to burn with a kind of imploding, brilliant fire. Many were resplendent with ornaments and glittering jewels, and some had their hair twisted into elaborate braids and spikes. But some of them looked quite ordinary, and in other circumstances she thought they might well have been her friends – if it had not been for the aura of darkness that surrounded them, of course.

One dark angel in particular caught her attention. He looked quite young still, hardly much more advanced than Josh and Bel, but he carried himself with a kind of arrogance and cruelty that seemed to mark him out from his fellows. He strutted round contemptuously and even aimed a kick at Fang, but he seemed nevertheless to be a favourite of Azariel's, because the Cherub laughed and summoned him over, then talked to him closely. Next instant he waved him away with an imperious sweep of the hand, and the young dark angel shot up and past the hidden Watchers, so close that Raffie could feel the breeze from his flight. Following the direction of her eyes, Raguel muttered, 'That's Tiercel, one of Azariel's chief lieutenants. A nasty piece of work. If you see him coming any time, get out of the way. He's trouble.'

Raffie could well believe it. Raguel now seemed to have seen as much as he wanted. He signalled to the Watchers to follow, and then took off in the opposite direction to that just taken by Tiercel. 'We've seen enough,' he said, gathering the Watchers around him as soon as they were safely out of range. 'We'll report back.' He looked at Raffie and added, 'And I think you'd better come with us, angel. Earth only knows how you managed to get through down there. Like Azariel said, you should have been picked up immediately by their surveillance, but they're most certainly keeping an eye out for you now, so you'd better come back with us till we decide what to do.'

They flew straight as arrows towards the Third Heaven, where Raffie knew the Watchers had their headquarters. Raguel set a pace that left her winded, a trail of blazing light fanning out behind him the only evidence of his flight, and Raffie knew that down on Earth the men and women who saw it would think they had seen a shooting star. But that was small consolation, because within moments she found she couldn't keep up, and she began to wish desperately that she were far enough advanced to have four wings instead of only the basic two. Seeing her plight, one of the Watchers took pity on her and caught her arm. 'Lean on me,' he said gruffly. 'The Commander always goes like the clappers. He forgets, you see, that not everyone can keep up. But we won't let you fall behind.'

They flew on. Raffie was rather annoyed. She was breathless and uncomfortable; this was not turning out to be the sort of holiday she had envisaged. She wondered briefly what Josh and Libertybel were doing and, not for the first time, began to regret that she had turned down the offer to go and have a look at Andromeda. Earth was beginning to feel a bit too dangerous, no matter what she did. As they shot up through the stratosphere and began their approach towards the entrance to Watcher HQ, Raffie noticed the unusually high number of combat angels pouring in and out through the main portals. And many, as she recognized from their markings, belonged to the Special Host Unit commanded by Raguel. 'Is this normal?' she shouted to the Watcher who was still towing her along.

He glanced at her briefly, a curious expression on his face, and shook his head. 'Not entirely. The Host have been put on alert. You'll find out all about it soon enough.'

They landed on a wide platform of billowing cloud, and Raffie was surprised to see Lucis standing chatting with a group of fellow Watchers over at the side, all of whom were rather battered and dishevelled, looking as if they might just have flown in from perimeter duty. 'Good Cosmos, Raffie!' Lucis exclaimed, catching sight of her and hurrying over as she found herself deposited none too gently on the platform. 'What have you been up to? I've been very worried.'

Raffie stared at him. The last person she had been expecting to see was her mentor, and she wondered how he had got there. Just then, however, Raguel came up and said heartily, 'Ah good, Lucis. We've brought your student safely back, as you can see. Do you want to join us for debriefing?'

Lucis nodded, springing smartly to attention. 'Yes, please, sir, if I may. I'm sorry I let her get caught up in all of that.'

The Cherub's face was a study. 'Ye-es,' he agreed. Then he gave him a wry smile. 'But I'm not sure there's much you could have done to stop her, if even half of what I've heard about this young angel is true.'

Raguel nodded abruptly and turned to leave. Realizing that Lucis must have been summoned before they arrived, Raffie pulled on her mentor's arm as he prepared to follow, and hissed, 'Lucis, what's going on? I don't understand. How did you *get* here? Is this your unit?'

Slightly irritated at being pulled back, Lucis snapped, 'No, Raffie.' His voice was low, and it was clear he didn't want to be overheard. 'I had a class A order from Raguel as they were bringing you back up. He said you had got involved in an incident, and that my presence here was required.'

Raffie's eyes widened. 'But why?' she protested. 'It's all over and I'm safe now, so what does it matter? What's all the fuss about?'

Lucis looked as if he didn't want to get into any of this at the moment. He sucked in his cheeks slightly, signalling to her to lower her voice, and said, 'Not now, Raffie.'

'But Lucis!' protested Raffie.

Seeing she was not going to let him go unless he told her, Lucis pulled a face and then muttered hurriedly, 'The fuss, Raffie, is that you seem to have blundered into the opening hostilities of an Enemy operation to gain complete control of one of the five continents down on Earth. They were being monitored by our side, and rumour has it that we're preparing to launch a counter-offensive in the very near future. That's why there are so many troops around at the moment. By appearing the way you did, however, you completely changed the existing power balance. The Enemy had put in place that man you saw… what's his name?'

'Nikolai?' supplied Raffie.

Lucis nodded. 'Yes, Nikolai, that's the one… Anyway, Azariel had put him in place under direct orders from Metatron, with instructions to start off a revolution that would overturn any influence we have in the area. His adoption as president of the country you landed on was supposed to be a foregone conclusion, but by appearing the way you did, just at the crucial moment, you turned people off the idea of a revolution and made them think about peace and trying to get on with each other.' Raffie looked blank, and Lucis continued patiently, 'You see, your unexpected presence down there affected the atmosphere, and now all the people who saw you are setting up a religious shrine. Pilgrims will be flocking there from all over the world, not to mention a whole cohort of priests. All of which, I might add, given that people will have to cross an Earth battle zone in order to get there, will be no mean feat.

'But the real problem now is that, as your appearance was completely without authorization, we've got no specific plans for follow up, so what do we do? Do we maintain this shrine, and put in place angelic backup – which may well commit us to long-term hostilities in that area, with the risk of casualties? And if we do that, do we then try to get authorization for a few more controlled visitations and minor miracles? Or do we temporarily withdraw from the area completely, as had been initially planned, and let the Enemy have a clean sweep, while we concentrate on putting together a counter-offensive that will rid the continent of Enemy occupation for good?'

He fell silent. Raffie was stunned. 'Gosh,' she managed at last. It had never even occurred to her that her appearance might have this sort of effect.

'Gosh indeed,' agreed Lucis wryly. 'Perhaps now you can appreciate that nothing ever happens in isolation, Raffie.'

But Raffie was still puzzled. She scratched her head and said slowly, 'But Lucis, if my appearance brought an end to this revolution that the Enemy wanted to start, that's good, isn't it?'

Lucis looked pained, as if she had somehow missed a vital point. 'Well yes, Raffie,' he agreed, 'to the extent that it has frustrated Enemy plans to destroy any influence we might have in the area. But no, when you think that any failure on our part to handle the situation properly now might lead to the most terrible chaos, not to mention division. And in the end, that could well mean that our plans to regain control of the area in the longer term might fail. Which, given that a lot of people and angels are likely to get hurt, as I am sure even you will appreciate, has got to be bad!'

9
The Heavenly Council

Raffie had never seen so much activity. She found herself in a long meeting with Raguel and the Watchers which Lucis was allowed to sit in on as an observer, and during which they went over in detail all that had happened. At the finish, Raguel sat back and said, 'There's nothing for it, I'm afraid. We're going to have to have a full heavenly Council meeting on this one. There's no knowing where it might end. We've got to lay the full facts before the King and let him decide.'

After that, there seemed to be a lot of scurrying round, with messengers flying out and replies coming back. Raffie felt rather lost and unimportant. It was so busy that she wondered if she might be able to creep away while no one was looking and maybe join Josh on Andromeda. Lucis, however, came in while she was sorting out the wing-enhancement boosters all trainees needed for unaccompanied cosmological perimeter flying (extra-long feathers that were attached to the shoulders, giving more power) and said sternly, 'If you think you're going anywhere, you can forget about it now. They'll want you to give testimony once the Council has been convened. After all, it's your fault all this started.'

There didn't seem any answer to this; Raffie hung her head, ashamed. It was true. How could she have even thought of creeping away? It was an uncomfortable kind of experience, nonetheless, waiting while all the preparations were made. The dignitaries streamed into the facility in an almost endless procession, from every corner of every universe and beyond. There were some very strange-looking angels among them, radiantly beautiful but in a form Raffie had never come across before. Some were covered entirely with feathers, wonderful long, sweeping plumes, but which made their wings and limbs seem almost joined. And others seemed almost formless but sparkled with a kind of jewel-like iridescence that made them hazy and hard to see. In the face of so much splendour, Raffie felt awestruck, and she began to realize that creation was a very, very large place, and she was only a very small part of it.

Then, however, just as Raffie was feeling hopelessly insignificant, Drizzlewobbel came in with a representative group from Weather, and he was so warm and so obviously pleased to see her that she felt slightly heartened. 'Hello, Raffie,' he said enthusiastically, his eye falling upon her as she loitered dejectedly at the back of the main entrance hall. 'Causing trouble again, are you?' But he didn't sound at all annoyed, which was what she had been worrying about. Then, as he registered her still drooping wings, he gave her a quick hug and whispered, 'Never mind. You couldn't have been there in the first place, you know, if His Majesty hadn't known. So don't take too much notice of the Cherubs. They don't know everything, despite what they say.' Then he smiled encouragingly and moved on.

Shortly after that Madame Germinel arrived too, wearing an amazing long floaty gown that seemed to sparkle and shimmer with every colour of the rainbow. 'Raffie!' she cried as she swept majestically down and settled on a banked cloud that obligingly puffed up around her like a throne. 'My little cabbage! 'Ow are you? I 'ave been so worried! Are you all right? They told me you 'ad been in the trouble!'

Raffie felt herself blush, her pleasure in once again seeing the formidable head of BABE somewhat dampened by the realization that her own part in the current crisis was now apparently common knowledge. She roused herself sufficiently, however, to smile sheepishly and say, 'I didn't realize you'd be here too. I thought it was only combat angels who were involved.'

Madame Germinel obviously thought this was ridiculous. 'But no, Raffie!' she cried dismissively. 'You clearly do not understand. The full Council has been called now. Everyone, but everyone, will be 'ere. And besides, my department is very important.' She bent lower and whispered, 'The babies you and Joshuel delivered, you remember?'

Raffie nodded blankly, puzzled by the abrupt change of subject, and Madame Germinel beamed. 'They are crucial!' she whispered again, glancing quickly round to make sure she wasn't overheard. 'One of them is to play a major part in the struggle that is to come.'

Not for the first time in conversation with Madame Germinel, Raffie began to feel totally confused. 'The struggle to come?' she repeated, bewildered. 'But I thought the whole point of this Council meeting was that no one had foreseen that any of this was going to happen?'

'Oh, tck!' Madame Germinel shook her head. 'No, Raffie, I am not talking about your hilltop and the localized trouble you 'ad. Bad though that was. I mean THE BIG STRUGGLE!' She rolled her eyes dramatically. 'It is coming soon, you know?'

Raffie did not know. She hadn't a clue. From all that Lucis had said earlier, she had thought that the Council was only just beginning to consider the matter, and that there were no concrete plans as yet in place. She didn't, however, think it was worth pursuing the point, because the more Madame Germinel said, the more lost Raffie became. So she smiled weakly instead, and was rewarded by a look of delight on Madame Germinel's face – as if all was now crystal clear. Then the Head of BABE swept on.

Just before the full meeting was convened, Lucis came and found her. 'Come with me, Raffie,' he said mysteriously, 'there's something I want you to see.'

The something, however, turned out to be someone. Or, more precisely, some two, because he led her a long way, down through what felt to be endless corridors, to a very small door, tucked away on the lowest level of the Mansion. There he paused and, still beaming mysteriously, very gently pushed it back. Raffie stepped forward and peered in – and then almost fell over with surprise, because there inside, waiting for her, stood Josh and Bel.

'Gosh!' she gasped, almost speechless with joy at coming across them again so unexpectedly. 'What are you two doing here? I thought you'd still be off roaming the Andromeda system and America!'

The two grinned, and Josh sprang forward and hugged

her. Then he stood back and exclaimed, 'We're really cross with you, Raffie!'

Beside him Bel ruffled his wings indignantly and said, 'Yeah, how could you go and have an adventure like that, and not take us?'

Raffie was so happy she felt she was going to explode. Nothing seemed to matter quite so much now she was back with her friends. 'But I didn't know!' she protested, laughing. 'I wasn't looking for an adventure. It just sort of crept up on me. I didn't even know Raguel was *there* till the imps went for me.'

Josh gave a low whistle, as if this last piece of information was news indeed, and said admiringly, 'Raguel? Wow, Raffie, you really know how to pick them. He's second in command of the elite, under Michael. Did you know?'

Raffie shook her head. Bel demanded, 'Didn't you even realize there was something big going down when you saw how quiet it was?'

But before she could reply, Lucis said firmly, 'I'm sorry to interrupt, but you're going to have to save all this till later. I have to take you all up to the Great Chamber now.' He smiled as Raffie looked at him enquiringly and added, 'Yes, yes, that's right. Gabriel thought you were feeling a bit lost in all the hubbub, you see. He's been taking a personal interest after all that's happened, and he said he could see you weren't happy, so he authorized me to bring these two back to keep you company while the Council was in session.'

Raffie gaped. To her knowledge she hadn't seen the archangel once since they had arrived, and to learn now that someone so exalted had been keeping an eye on her and, even more, was concerned about how she might be feeling, amazed her. But then again, she reflected, archangels were a rather amazing bunch all round, no matter how you looked at it. Quietly, together with Josh and Bel – both of whom, she was pleased to note, seemed equally as awestruck as she was – she followed Lucis up to the Great Chamber.

As they drew near, they heard music, and what sounded like a huge choir. 'It's the Seraphim,' explained Lucis, catching the startled expressions on their faces. 'Pretty good, aren't they? They always turn up when the King's around. He's very keen on that sort of thing.' He stared around worriedly, looking for a way through the thick crowds, and said, 'We really must be quick and take our seats. If that lot have started, it means His Majesty will be arriving any moment, and no one will be allowed in once he's taken his seat.'

Josh, Bel and Raffie exchanged looks. The very idea that they should be present at a full session of the Council held in the presence of the King seemed staggering. Junior angels didn't usually even get to see the King from a distance, and the Seraphim were famous, reputedly the best choir in all creation. 'Wow,' muttered Bel, more awestruck still, as they filed in behind Lucis. 'I've heard all about these guys from my mentor. He said they were great! But I never thought I'd ever get to hear them for myself. At least, not yet. Fantastic!'

The huge Great Chamber was packed. It was constructed like a Greek or Roman amphitheatre, with no roof, but extending infinitely up into the inky darkness of the heavens above. Below, row upon row of tiered seats rose steeply from the stage that stood at the centre, and these were now filling rapidly with the fabulous and exotic-looking angels who had been streaming in over the past days.

The Seraphim were on the left, a huge mass of them, and Raffie suddenly realized that they were the formless, glowing beings that she had seen before when she was hanging around the entrance hall. Only now, as they sang, they seemed to take shape, and at the centre of each shining mass she could see exquisite, beautiful beings with long flowing hair and calm faces that seemed to radiate an intense peace. She stopped, gaping at them in amazement. Behind her Josh gave a shove and hissed, 'Get a move on, Raffie. Lucis will really be cross if we lose him now.'

The Watcher confidently led the way down to the front. To her horror, Raffie realized that they were to be sitting directly at the foot of the great stage, clearly visible to the whole Council. 'Lucis,' she whispered urgently, catching him up and tugging at his sleeve, 'Are you sure this is right?'

He merely nodded and said, 'Quite sure, Raffie. Like I said, you're to give testimony.'

This, Raffie felt, was bad news. She had never dreamed her own contribution was going to be so public. Writhing with embarrassment, she slid into the seat Lucis gestured towards and then tried to squirm down out of sight, but it was no good. No matter how low she got, she found she could still be seen clearly from the tiers behind, and so she gave up and looked around instead. It was awesome, but she had no chance to take it all in, because at that moment there was a loud fanfare of trumpets, and the massed banks of angels rose to their feet. Then into the silence rippled a long clear note that fell like an announcement and was immediately picked up by the orchestra, which Raffie now discovered was situated in a deep well just in front of them. Then as the stately music throbbed out, there was a stir at the back of the chamber. Very slowly, a cloud that shimmered and blazed with spinning light, which seemed to have at its heart a fantastically jewelled floor, began to descend towards the stage.

As it came lower, Raffie could just make out in the middle four huge Cherubs, standing guard around what looked like a massive throne. But it was a throne like none Raffie had ever seen before. It looked to be made of the same shimmering jewels that paved the floor, and on it sat the most wonderful, beautiful individual Raffie had ever seen, wreathed in pulsating bands of brilliant light which made it difficult to see. Raffie stared and rubbed her eyes but, no matter how hard she tried, she found she still couldn't quite make the figure out. She was spell-bound.

The cloud came to a rest in the centre of the stage, and the four huge Cherubs each stepped forward, arms outstretched, holding in their hands two mighty swords which glittered in the light. All four were in full ceremonial dress; Raffie gasped, stunned at how impressive they seemed. She recognized one of them as Raguel, and her eyes widened even more. He had seemed splendid before, but it was nothing compared with the way he looked now. In the same instant, he caught her eye and inclined his head slightly in greeting, and, at her side, Bel gasped and muttered, 'I don't believe it. He just nodded at you, Raffie!'

Then, however, almost as if at a signal, the shimmering, rustling ranks of angels all sat down. From the midst of the iridescent waves of rainbow light surrounding the throne, the King raised a hand and silence fell. But it was a silence like none Raffie had ever experienced before, because it seemed like a living thing, filled with meaning. It wound its way inside her like little spiral-shaped shards of brightness, suggesting new worlds and undreamed-of possibility, all at once and all the time. With a thrill of excitement, she suddenly realized that she was hearing the Trisagion, the eternal song of creation that upheld all worlds and that came from the King himself.

At her side, Josh whispered, 'Wow…! Can you hear that?' He sounded stunned.

'Sssh!' hissed Lucis.

The Seraphim took up the refrain, and little bursts of light exploded throughout the darkness overhead. 'Gosh, they're stars,' breathed Bel, ignoring the Watcher. 'New stars! They're being created… NOW!'

The look Lucis threw on them would have withered a lesser-eyed boggle imp at ten paces – and they were known throughout the heavens for being particularly disruptive. 'For heaven's sake, be quiet!' he admonished. 'I won't tell you again!'

The opening preliminaries over, Raguel came before the throne and began to make his report. He spoke firmly, his voice carrying without any effort to the farthest corners of the Great Chamber. While he was speaking, Raffie kept glancing nervously around, aware that it would very soon now be her own turn. The prospect filled her with dread. She had no idea how many angels were there, but it looked to her to be in the tens of thousands at least, and the idea of standing up before all of them and recounting what had happened made her wings turn to jelly.

But, as Raguel continued with his report, she found herself becoming increasingly absorbed in what he was saying. He started off by detailing recent developments in what he called 'the Enemy offensive', unemotionally describing a series of heavy combat losses in various engagements that had taken place over the whole of Earth. Then he went on to summarize intelligence reports that had been received, all of which pointed to the start of a major Enemy strategy in eastern Europe, being masterminded by Azariel, and involving a certain rebel leader called Nikolai.

As the angels listened, it was clear to Raffie that none of this was exactly news to any of them. From all sides there were unsurprised nods, and then at last Raguel came to the meeting on the hilltop and began to relate what had happened. When he began to describe Nikolai, angels throughout the vast amphitheatre sat forward in their seats, listening intently as if keen to absorb every detail. Then, holding out his hand, from which there now poured a thin stream of light, Raguel projected a three-dimensional image of the man onto the cleared area of stage before the throne. There were low 'aaahs' as angels scrutinized the man and took in every detail of his appearance. After that, from all sides, angels began to ask questions. 'What's his background?' called one. 'How firmly under the control of the Enemy is he?' enquired another.

Raguel waved them all aside impatiently. 'As we had suspected,' he said bluntly, 'his allegiance to the Enemy seems total. But that is no surprise, and is not the reason for summoning this Council meeting.' He beckoned Raffie to come forward and said loudly, 'As you will, I am sure, already have heard, there has been an unexpected and unforeseen development. A totally new ingredient has been added that has changed the situation as it now stands drastically. It is the duty of the Council here gathered to decide how we need to respond.'

He held up a hand to stop the wave of excited chatter that had broken out and then, having first bowed to the throne, he took a firm grip on Raffie's shoulder and drew her forward. 'I wish to present to you all Raffael. This young angel somehow – and don't ask me how, because I don't know – managed to bypass all Enemy surveillance and penetrated unnoticed right to the heart of the Enemy operation. And while there, as Nikolai was speaking – and, as had been foreseen, was inciting the people to rebel – she materialized in full view of the crowd.'

A shocked silence greeted this announcement. Someone called out, 'Was she seen?'

Raguel gave a wry smile. 'It would have been difficult for her not to have been. She appeared directly above Nikolai's head and… wait a minute, I'll show you.'

He raised an arm, pointing his finger, and onto the floor of the stage – replacing Nikolai – there now appeared another image. Raffie once more saw the hilltop, thronged with people, all listening intently as the revolutionary leader appeared and began to speak. It was almost as if she were there, and Raffie felt a trickle of fear as she once more heard the sullen mutters of the crowd, slowly growing in volume. Then, just as Raguel had said,

Raffie appeared on the rock above Nikolai's head, body hunched forward as she strained to hear, while a wave of black, jabbering imps seemed to explode out of nowhere and then hurtle across the short stretch of grassy slope.

In the chamber, pandemonium broke out, and again Raguel had to hold up his arm for quiet. 'Angels,' he cried. 'Please...! All your questions will be answered, but now allow Raffael to describe the incident as she saw it. She has things to add that you *must* hear.'

In the silence that followed, Raguel gave Raffie a small shove. She stumbled forward into the centre of the stage, directly in front of the throne. 'Go on,' encouraged Raguel as she hesitated. 'They're not going to eat you. They just want to hear your version of what happened.'

Abashed, Raffie stole a quick look from under her eyelashes up at the packed rows of seats. It was a mistake. Rank upon rank of shining angel faces stared back down at her, and for a moment it was all Raffie could do not to turn around and flee. She was saved only by the thought that, if she did, she would find herself face to face with the King. And Raffie didn't feel she was quite ready for that experience yet.

She glanced at Josh for reassurance and saw him grin encouragingly and nod his head. It was all she needed. Taking a deep breath, she began falteringly to relate what had happened. But just as she got to the part where she had first seen the hill, and was describing how she had been intrigued by sight of the crowds streaming towards the summit, there was a loud bang from outside the chamber, followed by a frightened cry.

Startled, Raffie froze, and everyone turned and stared

towards the great doors. There were more shouts and the sounds of a scuffle. Then there was a sudden blinding flash of light, and the doors exploded back as if ripped apart by a giant hand.

In the confusion that followed, all that could be seen were clouds of billowing black smoke and, all around, angels began to retch and cough as a horrible acrid smell of burning filled the air. As the fumes began to clear, a sinister figure appeared in the doorway. There were gasps of astonishment from all sides and then, as the last remaining wisps of smoke cleared away, Raffie made out the most fearsome angel she had ever seen, his face dark as death.

10
An Unwelcome Visitor

The figure strolled nonchalantly forward through the last remaining wisps of smoke and began to descend slowly towards the stage. Standing where she was, just in front of the throne, Raffie had an almost perfect view. She saw before her a massive angel, easily bigger than Raguel – and maybe even than Gabriel too – with a dark, proud face and flashing eyes. His four wings were a glossy blue-black, edged with silver, and he wore dark, polished armour that hinted at battle and cruelty. But most startling of all was the aura he seemed to give off. Whereas all the angels that Raffie had so far come across had been surrounded by brilliant light, this angel seemed rather, from the inner recesses of his terrifying body, to emanate inky, mind-disintegrating, chaotic darkness.

He was truly terrifying. Raffie heard Lucis gasp and then mutter, 'It's Metatron, the Prince Regent! Now there'll be trouble.'

Lucis's reaction seemed to be echoed throughout the chamber. Angels and archangels alike had all turned and were staring upwards ashen-faced, but the threatening figure staring arrogantly back down seemed unconcerned. He paused, his eyes flicking around, then began to stroll carelessly down the main aisle towards the throne, a small troop of equally fearsome dark Cherubs and Tempters close at his back. He walked as if he were a rival King, demanding respect as of right from all sides. Standing all alone on the stage, Raffie could only watch his approach helplessly. Paralysis seemed to have seized her limbs. Then the unthinkable happened. Ten paces away the dark angel stopped, and his cat-like eyes flickered and then fixed on her inquisitively.

Raffie had the sudden and terrifying sensation of plummeting into a bottomless pit. She felt her knees buckle and thought that she was going to fall. Then, into the darkness that surrounded her, she heard a quiet voice say, 'It's all right. Move, Raffie. Don't rush... Just go back to your seat.'

The words were like a lifeline, tossed out as she was sucked into the darkness, drawing her back. She grasped at them thankfully, finding in their quiet tone the strength to wrench her mesmerized gaze away from those horrific eyes. Slowly, and as if she were battling against a terrible force, she turned her head and discovered Raguel standing beside her. The tall Cherub was now partially screening her, his eyes fixed on the dark angel before them, a grim expression on his face. He did not look down as Raffie turned, but she felt his protection extending out across her like a shield. In the same instant the Cherub raised his two swords as a warning and said aloud, 'Hold, Prince. You have no right of access here.'

A look of contempt settled on the Regent's face, but at least his attention was no longer fixed upon Raffie, and she stumbled as he looked aside, half falling as if he had physically released her. Then the feeling began to return to her limbs. Almost crying with relief, she looked up and found Lucis staring at her, willing her to move. Slowly, her legs like lead, Raffie began to heave herself painfully back towards her seat, eyes still glued to Lucis's face. It seemed so far... Then, just as she felt she couldn't manage another step, the Watcher's hands reached out and grabbed her, and she was yanked to safety.

Raffie realized she was trembling violently, and for a moment felt too distraught to take in what was happening. But after a while, she managed to raise her head and look up, and her eyes widened in disbelief as she took in the scene now being played out before the throne.

As if not quite able to believe the evidence of his eyes, the Regent uttered a short bark of mirthless laughter, then shrugged disdainfully and made a move to go on. Instantly Raguel stepped forward and seemed to swell with menace, while the light flashed off his glittering swords. But he was all alone, and behind the Regent there was a terrible grating sound as the dark angels too now drew out their weapons and came forward to surround their leader. Raffie was petrified. She was convinced that Raguel was about to be cut down by the oncoming angels, right there in front of the throne. Suddenly, however, from the Seraphim over on the left, there sounded a long clear note. It fell into the atmosphere of growing dark like a shaft of pure light, and the three other Cherubs who had been standing guard with Raguel stepped forward and took their place at his side, forming a wall of opposition.

This appeared to be unexpected for the Prince Regent because he checked, his eyes flashing, then barked, 'Would you oppose me, Raguel?'

The Cherub did not hesitate. 'Yes, Lord,' he replied. 'I bar your approach to the King.'

For a moment it looked as if there was going to be a full scale fight, right there on the steps leading to the throne, but then, just as the Tempters again moved forward, swords raised and menace oozing from every last wing feather, a lone figure suddenly walked out in front of the Cherubs and commanded, 'Hold! Put up your swords, all of you.'

It was so unexpected that an audible gasp went up from the assembled angels, and Raffie was riveted. She had never seen anyone like this before. He was not an angel, because he didn't have wings, but she wasn't sure what he was. She saw a being who looked a little bit like some of the men and women she had come across down on Earth, wearing a simple white robe and with long, flowing golden hair and a beard. But there the similarity ended, because this being was tall and indescribably beautiful, and radiated the same kind of power and intense, pulsating light that flowed from the throne. He had no wings, it was true, but the authority he gave off nevertheless appeared to dominate everything all around. And suddenly, by contrast, the Regent didn't seem so big any more.

Now the strange being walked farther forward into the space between the two opposing groups, the air around him crackling softly, and stood directly in front of the Regent, eyeing him in silence.

'Lucis,' whispered Raffie, overcome with curiosity and unable to contain herself any longer, 'who is he?'

'Hush,' whispered the Watcher. 'It's the Crown Prince. Don't you recognize him?' As Raffie's eyes looked as if they were about to fall out of her head, he hurriedly continued, 'He speaks directly for the King and commands all our forces, and the Regent would like to depose him. Only he's never been strong enough.'

Raffie felt even more bewildered. 'But the Regent's an angel...' she began, 'and the Crown Prince... what *is* he?'

'He's the King's son,' whispered back Lucis. 'Like I just said! And you're right... He's not an angel at all, so he doesn't need wings or anything. He's powerful enough without them. But ssssh! We'll miss what's going on.'

The solitary and awe-inspiring figure raised his hand gently and said, 'What is it you want here, Prince?'

In response, the dark angel glowered. He seemed to be fighting some sort of internal battle, but at last he managed to get a hold of himself and spat, 'You know as well as I do what I want! I want to know what's going on. Why have your forces been interfering down on Earth?'

The Crown Prince raised an eyebrow and repeated, 'Interfering?'

'Yes,' snarled back the Regent. 'Precisely. I know that BABE has tried to infiltrate an agent...'

'Hardly an agent,' interrupted the Crown Prince. 'I should remind you that Earth remains a full part of the Cosmos, and the King decides...'

'Not without my agreement, he doesn't!' snapped back the archangel furiously. 'I was appointed Regent. Don't you remember? Your father himself gave me authority over Earth, to govern it as I saw fit. And that still hasn't been revoked.'

A steely glint came into the Crown Prince's eye, but his tone remained quiet. 'As I remember,' he said calmly, 'my father gave you authority to govern Earth *in his name*. But you've rather gone beyond that, haven't you? The planet has become a byword throughout the Cosmos for trouble and rebellion. You're only still in place because removing you now would destroy half the creatures down there before they've had a chance to realize what's going on and save themselves from judgment!'

The Regent chose to ignore the latter part of this. 'The fact remains,' he hissed back, 'that you and the Council have been plotting behind my back, trying to undermine my legitimate right to control the planet as I see fit. I know that you've got an agent about to be born down there – and we'll find him, don't you worry! But that's not my only issue, as you very well know. In fact, that's why this Council is meeting here, if I'm not much mistaken, and I'm here to protest.

'I would remind you that my plans for planetary war were agreed by this respectable body itself,' Metatron sneered, 'in full accordance with Cosmic Law. And it's you who're now breaking that law by interfering!'

His wings fluffed out in fury, and the Tempters nearest him ducked their heads. He ignored them. 'There was never even a hint of authorization for angelic visitation,' he shouted. 'How you can have imagined for one moment that you could get round that by using a non-commissioned angel and a pathetic story about a mistake, I do not know. It's an act of Cosmic War!'

With horror, Raffie realized that they were talking about her. Of course, she knew her unexpected materialization had caused a problem, but she'd had no idea it might cause a row on this scale. Cosmic War? Her idiocy couldn't possibly lead to that. She tried to step forward, wanting to say something to correct the Regent's mistake, but Lucis restrained her. The Crown Prince replied evenly, 'Let me assure you, Regent, the materialization *was* a mistake.'

But this only further inflamed the Regent. 'Mistake?' he shouted. 'The King doesn't allow mistakes. You know that as well as I do. There can't possibly have been a mistake!'

Meanwhile, Raffie suddenly had the strangest feeling that she was being watched. It was bizarre, like something cold and hard being aimed at her. She shifted uncomfortably and looked round, trying to pinpoint the direction from which it came. But there was nothing. She glanced at the dark angels clustered around the Regent and saw Azariel, his face contorted with hate. But it wasn't him, because his eyes were fixed on the Crown Prince. And then her eyes travelled on to a dark young angel standing over at the side, a little separate from the rest of the group. He was staring at her intently, a small smile playing about his lips, and Raffie recognized him instantly – Tiercel, the young Tempter she had seen down on the hill.

As their eyes locked, his smile spread; then he nodded his head slightly as if in salute and looked away. Raffie felt as if she had just flown through the ice wastes in space that separate different galaxies. In that moment she knew instinctively that Tiercel had somehow targeted her – whether or not because he recognized her she had no idea, but she knew that he had marked her out and that, whatever he was thinking, it was not good.

Down on the stage, however, and as if at last losing patience, the Crown Prince suddenly exploded.

'Enough, Metatron! You keep on talking about 'legitimate' authority, but was it 'legitimate' when you set up this man Nikolai? You're alleging some kind of plot, but nothing compares with what *you've* been trying to do!'

With difficulty, Raffie dragged her attention back, as there was a low rumble of angry agreement from the Council. The Regent glared round at them, then narrowed his eyes and said malevolently, 'Whatever I do, I do by right. My orders were to test these miserable Earth creatures and see where their loyalties lie. The means were left to me, and if I choose now to use this man Nikolai, what's it got to do with you? He's simply a tool. Nothing more, and nothing less. I've done nothing wrong. Your own father gave the orders for this. And if he wants to revoke them now, let him say so for himself!'

The Regent had issued a challenge, and all around there was shocked silence. Raffie understood perfectly. It had all been explained to them in angel school when she first started training. The King's voice was so powerful, their tutor in Astronomical Creation Studies had explained, that the last time it had been heard directly, the foundations of one of the smaller universes had cracked from end to end, with the result that all the planetary systems that were a part of it had had to be stripped back to their core elements so that the foundations could be rebuilt. And even then, their tutor had added mournfully, three very nasty black holes had opened up which had caused the most appalling trouble for ages afterwards, so in the end a specialist Watcher unit that dealt with that sort of thing had had to be brought in to seal them off. So these days, unless the matter was *really* serious, the King tended to speak through his son – which was much safer, and didn't carry the same risks. Metatron's words, therefore, were hugely insulting because they implied that the King had somehow lost power.

Now it was the turn of the Crown Prince to look angry. 'Yes,' he barked back, ignoring the insult, 'but your orders were to test humans in order to help them develop – to help them see the choices that were available to them so that they could distinguish right from wrong and choose the future for themselves. Not to destroy them and take control!'

The Regent's only reply was to shrug with contempt and turn away. 'It's not my fault they're so weak,' he said dismissively.

But this was apparently too much. The Crown Prince shouted, 'Don't turn your back on me, Metatron. I know what you're up to! You're a liar and a thief! You've been working away at this from the beginning, trying to take control. But you've gone too far with all these lies! You're not King on Earth and you never will be! You can't keep on trying to hide behind the law.'

'So stop me,' flung back the Regent over his shoulder. 'If you dare!'

A ripple of unease ran round the amphitheatre, and the Tempters who were gathered around Metatron smirked. The Crown Prince, however, hadn't finished. 'All right,' he replied, dangerously quiet. 'I will.' The words stung the air with menace. 'Your arrogance has gone far enough.'

The Regent's reaction was immediate. He jerked back round, hand flying to his sword, and the Cherubs all immediately sprang forward, forming a line of defence in front of the Crown Prince, who was unarmed. Then, however, something extraordinary and, to Raffie at least, unexpected happened.

While this exchange had been going on, the figure on the throne had remained almost invisible, wreathed in numinous bands of sparkling cloud. But now there was a sudden movement. Raffie wasn't sure, but she felt, rather than saw, the King rise to his feet. There was a blaze of light, then a shock wave of pure power blasted through the air. Metatron leapt back as if he'd been bitten. Simultaneously the Crown Prince glanced backwards, and in the splitting of a celestial atom some sort of instant exchange seemed to take place between him and his father.

He turned back to the Regent and declared, 'This means war, Metatron.'

The statement hung in the air, and the Regent flinched. He seemed dazed, but swallowed and hissed balefully, 'Very well, if that's the way you want to play it. War it is! But don't forget, I still rule the Earth by right, and I'll defend that to extinction – of myself and the whole universe, if need be!'

Then, without more ado, he spun on his heel, signalling to the others to follow, and swept back up the stairs and out.

11
Off to Combat School

There was stunned silence, and then a hubbub broke out, with angels all round crying to be heard. It was a while before order could be restored, but the Crown Prince signalled to the Cherubs to return to their posts, and at last some sort of peace fell across the chamber. He waited until there was complete quiet, and then withdrew to the sparkling clouds now surrounding the throne to talk to the King.

When he emerged he looked grave. Moving slowly, he once again took up position on the centre of the stage, and stared round at the sea of faces. He seemed to be weighing something in his mind and as his eyes swept the chamber, they briefly rested on Raffie.

It was only the briefest of glances, but of course in eternity everything happens all at once and all the time, and in that instant Raffie felt as if he was scrutinizing every angelic particle of her being – including bits she'd have preferred to keep hidden. She blushed and he gave a slight smile, then his eyes swept on. He began to speak.

The Crown Prince had one of the most extraordinary voices Raffie had ever heard. When he'd spoken to Metatron his tone had seemed to resonate with power, not exactly angry, but truly awesome, and the air had seemed to shiver. Yet now, to Raffie, it sounded more like ripples of clear, sparkling water bubbling across rocks in a celestial stream, and she found her mind filled with images and scenes from a thousand different created worlds, all at the same time. She gave a slight gasp, knowing she was catching a glimpse of what their old Cosmology teacher in first school had called 'the realm of potentiality' – what he'd explained as 'the might have beens' and the 'could bes' of creation, all mixed up. At her side Lucis said, 'Ssh!' and raised a finger to his lips.

The Prince began by repeating the facts as they'd happened. But this time he emphasized how Raffie had blundered into a situation she couldn't possibly have understood, and how events had run away with themselves. Raffie felt oddly comforted, but the angels all around looked grave. 'So what are we going to do with her?' called out one. 'And what about this shrine?' shouted another. 'Does the King want it to be maintained, or what? How does it alter things?'

The questions popped back and forth like an out-of-control meteor, and for a moment it looked as though chaos was once again going to erupt, but then the Prince held up his hand for silence. 'You're absolutely right,' he said firmly, his voice carrying without effort to the farthest corners of the vast auditorium. 'This is exactly the problem. What do we do with the shrine? Current reports say that people are flocking there in their thousands. If we don't maintain it now, given that people don't seem inclined to let it go, we'll be leaving the way open for Metatron, and he'll use it for enormous harm.'

There were more cries all round. Some of the angels were horrified, some were angry. At last one stately archangel rose to his feet. 'My Lord,' he called, clearing his throat – rather pompously, Raffie thought, but it did at least succeed in silencing all the other angels. 'My Lord, from all you say, it seems clear we *must* maintain this shrine. To do anything less would be irresponsible. But rather than transfer other angels already engaged in important work elsewhere, I would suggest that the young angel who first caused the problem be given the task of looking after it. Starting immediately.'

With that he sat down. Raffie became aware of Lucis hopping up and down at her side, like a red giant star about to explode. The huge Watcher was waving all four wings and both hands in protest in what felt to Raffie like a mini tornado. 'My Lord!' he cried out, swirls of air flying in every direction. 'My Lord...'

Raffie, Josh and Bel all ducked. From the murmurs behind it was clear Lucis wasn't the only one wanting to have his say. 'Sit down, angel!' commanded a voice behind.

Lucis ignored it. 'I must protest,' he exclaimed. 'Raffael has been in my charge ever since her first term in school, and I feel I must speak for her...'

'Are you her mentor?' interrupted the Prince.

Lucis nodded. 'Yes, my Lord. I'm Lucis, and I've seen all her skylarking and every scrape that she's ever fallen into, but she's never intended any wrong. On the contrary: her real problem is enthusiasm!'

He launched into a long and tortuous description of Raffie's passion for Earth. She was mad about it, he explained, always had been. But the trouble was, she didn't know anything about it and, that being so, she couldn't possibly be put in charge of anything as important as a shrine. It would be a complete and utter disaster!

Raffie ruffled her feathers with indignation. But the angel who'd suggested she look after the shrine was now looking at her with an air of sympathy, as if this was news indeed, so she nodded in agreement and tried to look meek. Lucis's next words, however, stunned her. It wasn't just that she'd be useless, he insisted, but he strongly suspected, from the way the Regent had reacted, that Enemy forces from now on would be on the lookout for her. They quite clearly hadn't believed in her innocence, whatever the Crown Prince might have said, and therefore she'd be seen as a threat and targeted. In such circumstances it would be entirely wrong to allow her to return to Earth.

Poor Raffie thought her wing feathers were going to fall out with horror. Not be allowed back to Earth! What was Lucis talking about? She'd thought he was on her side!

Her mentor, however, *still* hadn't finished. 'As I see it,' he continued loudly – rather too loudly, judging by the way the angels sitting nearby winced, 'we're left with two choices. Either Raffie is assigned somewhere else completely – a music group maybe, or administration. Somewhere she'll be safe. Or...' He drew a deep breath. 'Or we decide to bypass her intermediate terrestrial studies completely, and send her immediately for first level combat training...'

Up on the fourth tier there was a sound like a boggle-eating imp erupting through the Milky Way. This was a particularly nasty sound as all angels knew, because boggle-eating imps weren't supposed to leave the secure zone round their proper galaxy, where they couldn't do much harm. When they did try and leave, therefore, all sorts of alarms went off, and those round the Milky Way – which was a favourite escape route – were especially bad.

Outraged, Madame Germinel sprang to her feet. 'But, Lucis,' she screeched, staring down at him in horror, 'the little one is not experienced enough for that! You are crazy. She 'as not even begun training school yet. Look at 'er!' She pointed a finger quivering with indignation, for a moment incapable of going on. Then she cried, 'She is not one of your big rough tough fighters. She is... 'ow you say... DELICATE!'

'No, she's not!' flared back Lucis, stunned at being so rudely interrupted. 'She's no more delicate than you!' Madame Germinel's not inconsiderable chest swelled with offence, and he hurriedly continued, 'She's not some kind of celestial orchid, you know, whatever you might think. She'd never have coped with even half the things she has if she weren't "tough", as you put it. No!' He turned back to face the Council and pleaded, 'If you don't recommend her for training now, she won't stand a chance. It's unusual, I know, but whatever she looks like she's a natural for combat... So I would like to propose that she be transferred immediately.'

Silence greeted this at first, then all over the chamber angels turned to one another and began to discuss the matter. Raffie held her breath, too stunned even to move. A wild thrill of excitement had shot through her with Lucis's last words. Combat School! It was what every young angel dreamed of, though she'd never heard of basic training being skipped or curtailed before. In the natural course of things she should have gone on to second level school – in her case, down on Earth – and then had to have sat all the exams. She could hardly believe her ears.

Raffie stared round wide-eyed, wondering what the Council would decide, and suddenly realized that the Prince was staring at her, an expression of deep thought on his brow. What the object of his musings might be was impossible to tell, but he beckoned her forward and she went, trembling, with the sudden awful feeling that her little bubble of excitement was about to be well and truly burst. They weren't going to send her to Combat School. Of course not! Why should they? After all, whatever Lucis said, it was all her fault they were in this mess.

However, as if reading her thoughts, the Prince smiled at her and said softly, 'Just wait.' Then he laid a reassuring hand on her shoulder, and turned back to face the Council. Raffie felt as if she had inadvertently swallowed a bowl of star dust. A great surge of power seemed to flow through the Prince's fingers, and just for an instant she felt as if she were looking through eyes that weren't her own. She felt huge, as if she were gazing out over several different star-spangled universes all at the same time, and as if she could change creation at the flick of a thought. Then his hand dropped and the moment passed.

At long last, after what seemed forever – which, given that angels feel everything all at once and all the time, was an exceedingly long time – a Cherub sitting right at the back of the chamber stood up and called down, 'We would like to ask, my Lord, what is to happen about this Earth child the Regent mentioned? Does it in fact exist? And, if it does, will it be affected at all by what now happens with this shrine?'

The Prince frowned, and Raffie had the distinct impression that he had wanted to avoid this subject. But he merely nodded and said, 'Yes, I can confirm that the child exists, but more than that at the moment – for the success of the operation, and the child's safety – I'd rather not say. I would, however, add that precautions are in place to keep the child hidden. And they'll remain that way until such time as secrecy becomes no longer possible. But you're right, what happens with the shrine may well influence that, because the mood on Earth will be strongly affected.'

There was another low murmur at this, and Raffie realized that the Prince was once again staring at her. He seemed to come to a decision. 'Angels, I realize that some of the facts revealed today have come as a surprise to many of you, but the fate of this young angel *does* require attention, and we mustn't take too long. For better or worse, all that Lucis has said is true. Because of what's happened she will, from now on, be singled out for special attention by the Enemy. They *will* target her if and when she returns to Earth…'

Raffie held her breath. Here it comes, she thought, he's going to transfer me to Pluto or something. I'm never going to get back to Earth again now.

But the Prince frowned slightly and glanced back towards the throne – as if seeking confirmation – then nodded and carried on more slowly, weighing every word. 'As a matter of priority, therefore, I too feel that Raffael should now receive combat training. We must do whatever we can to arm her against attack... So, after consultation with my father, I've decided to accept Lucis's proposal. As of now I give permission for her to bypass intermediate training and proceed immediately to Combat School.' He turned to Raffie and said solemnly, 'Raffael, do you agree to this? I must warn you that it'll be hard there. So if you prefer, you can ask now for me to reassign you, and we'll find something less dangerous.'

His tone was ominous, and Raffie swallowed nervously. Over by Lucis, she saw Josh and Bel were both goggling at her with excitement, and Bel's lips formed a round 'O' of envy. Raffie felt afraid. She stared beyond the Prince to the rows of angels sitting behind. A deep silence settled over the chamber as everyone waited for her reply. Can I do it? she wondered. She felt a sudden moment of doubt and then, casting a quick glance back down, she saw Lucis nod encouragingly, as if he knew what was passing through her mind. Yet behind, Madame Germinel was still looking as if she were about to explode and Raffie's uncertainty increased. This must be serious, she knew, for the Head of BABE to look so disturbed.

Then all the stories Raffie had ever heard about Combat School flooded into her mind. How tough it was, the accident rate, and how hard it was to get in... And in that moment, Raffie knew that she wanted this more than anything else, no matter how hard it was.

She drew herself up, her mind made up, and saw the Prince smile. He looked like he already knew what she was about to say. Raffie didn't flinch. 'My Lord,' she began. She cast another quick look over at Josh and Bel, and then said more firmly, 'My Lord, I would love to go to

Combat School. I know how hard it is, but I've thought of nothing else ever since I began training and it's what I've always dreamed of… to become a Watcher, like Lucis. But there is one thing I would like to ask…'

The Prince had been about to speak, but he stopped at that and looked at her narrowly. 'Speak on, Raffael,' he said.

It was all or nothing, Raffie decided. She took a deep breath. 'My Lord,' she began, 'I would like to ask that my two friends, Joshuel and Libertybel, also be assigned for training. I could never have managed anything,' she went on, a trifle breathlessly, 'if they hadn't been with me. And they're much more advanced than me anyway. I think they're ready for it…'

She came to a stop as an expression of amusement settled on the Prince's face, but he said solemnly, 'I see.' Then he looked over to where Josh and Bel were both standing. 'Joshuel and Libertybel, come here.' They came forward nervously to take their places beside Raffie, and the Prince surveyed them, the expression on his face unreadable. 'You've heard what your friend has asked,' he said at last. 'But how do you both feel? Are you ready for the discipline of Combat School? Would you be willing to undertake it?'

Beside her, Josh and Bel could hardly contain themselves. 'Yes, my Lord,' they both managed, and Josh's wings gave a little flutter of excitement that he seemed absolutely unable to repress.

The Prince smiled. 'So be it then,' he announced. 'The three of you will go immediately!' Then he raised his arms and cried, 'Angels, from this moment on the Regent is barred all right of access to this Council, and is declared Enemy to the King. Our agent is already in place on Earth and must now grow to maturity. Our task for the present is to keep the child hidden. Meanwhile, these three young angels will be trained so that they can join us in the coming fight. And at the right moment – the appointed moment – we'll take Metatron on. We'll defeat him once and for all and take back Earth as our own!' He gave a great shout, raising his hand. 'Are you with me?'

From all sides, the host of angels and archangels sprang to their feet and the star-spangled vaults above reverberated to a wild cheer. 'Yes!' they shouted. 'To battle and victory! Let us take back Earth as our own!'

Staring up at them all, Raffie felt a thrill of excitement. She knew that enormous and terrible trials might lie ahead, but she was still convinced that they would win. They might not all survive, it was true – and maybe she, Josh and Bel would be amongst those who were lost. But, led by the Crown Prince, she couldn't believe Metatron would prevail. She looked round and found Josh and Bel both staring at her eagerly. 'We're going to be a part of it all, Raffie,' breathed Josh. 'We're going to be commissioned into the Host!'

'Yeah,' agreed Bel with a grin. 'And then let the Regent watch out. We'll kick him out of the sky!'

Raffie was almost too overcome to speak. She nodded her head vigorously. 'Yes,' she agreed. 'But best of all... we're going to do it together!'

All Lion books are available from your local bookshop, or can be ordered via our website or from Marston Book Services. For a free catalogue, showing the complete list of titles available, please contact:

Customer Services
Marston Book Services
PO Box 269
Abingdon
Oxon
OX14 4YN

Tel: 01235 465500
Fax: 01235 465555

Our website can be found at:
www.lionhudson.com